THE COVERT GUARDIAN

LIANE ZANE

ZEPHON ROMANCE

Digital Edition JULY 2023 ISBN: 979-8-9850781-1-4

Print Edition ISBN: 979-8-9850781-6-9

Cover design by Betelgeuse, 99Designs

ONE

D espite the warm powdery sand between her toes, the vast blue sky overhead, and the crystalline Mediterranean as far as she could see, Olivia Markham might as well have been in prison or a hospital bed for all the fun she was having. A dull ache threatened her head even though she wore sunglasses against the glare and barely sipped the Sex on the Beach cocktail that her boyfriend Jamie had handed her with an exaggerated leer.

Said boyfriend was already on his second cocktail, and it was only two in the afternoon.

Olivia sighed. Drinking copious amounts of alcohol had been one of their primary missions in coming to Ibiza, the Spanish island known as the clubbing capital of the universe. At twenty, they couldn't even drink legally back home in the United States, but the legal drinking age in Spain was only 16—and most started even younger. In fact, there was a large gaggle of what looked like middle-schoolers down by a rugged outcrop of rocky shore. They had plastic cups in their hands, and the unpredictable way that they lurched and laughed told her that they weren't drinking soda.

Frowning, she sipped the sweet peach-, orange-, and cranberry-infused vodka drink.

Jamie placed a consoling palm on her bare shoulder. "Babe, what's wrong? Not enough simple syrup in your Sex on the Beach?" He waggled his eyebrows in case she didn't get his clumsy effort at innuendo.

"No, it's good," she said before glancing around at the milling swimsuit-clad tourists who clamored for tiki cocktails with tiny paper umbrellas and maraschino cherries jammed on miniature plastic cutlasses. "Something's just off."

Jamie gently tugged her chin until her gaze met his. "Hey, that's why we're here, right? To put the past in the past and let go and live a little? It's what Emily would have wanted for you."

Olivia's frown deepened. "No, that's not what I meant, Jame." She rubbed the small pewter medal hanging on a fine-gauge silver chain on her chest, which had grown hot in the midday sun. It nearly burned her fingertips. "That creeping sensation is making the hairs on the back of my arms stand up, like there's static electricity around us."

"Your spidey sense is tingling again?" Jamie asked this lightly enough, but Olivia could still hear traces of exasperated affection in his voice. More exasperation than affection, she suspected.

She couldn't blame him. He'd been patient during the past year at Brown University where they'd met in the premed program, but she'd been predicting disaster on this trip since before they boarded the plane back at Logan Airport.

Olivia sat up, her fingers curling around the medal in reflex. The sense of warning only increased. She swallowed, setting her barely touched Sex on the Beach onto the side table next to her lounge chair. "Yes."

Jamie bent and unwrapped her fingers from the embossed disc. "Seems like your gut is linked to this bizarre pendant. It's not even a proper piece of jewelry. Why do you still wear it?"

A low-grade buzz filled Olivia's ears. She didn't know if it was Jamie's question or the almost-visible vibrations pulsing through the air toward them from the southeast side of the beach. Several people pushed through a loose clump of young women, their faces stark with what looked very much like terror. The women yelled at these inconsiderate newcomers, with more than one throwing the contents of their cups at them. Instead of the predictable fight, the hurrying individuals only picked up their pace at an open stretch of sand. They didn't actually seem to be heading anywhere in particular, just *away from* the southeast.

"Hey, did you hear me?" asked Jamie, his sharply rising voice cutting through the buzzing.

Olivia looked at him. She let the weight of her unease keep her voice low. "Let's get out of here."

Anger sparked in Jamie's blue eyes. "What? We only just got here. I haven't even gotten into the water yet."

Olivia ignored his complaint and stood. Alarm shot through her as more people began to shove in a visible human wave through the people talking and laughing on the sand around them. It was too early and too calm for a spontaneous drunken crush to overtake the beach club, even if most of the people here had been drinking for days, only stopping to pass out in a dreamless stupor each night before getting up and doing it all again.

Olivia's suddenly sensitive hearing noted the babble of panic riding on the air towards them. A curious *rat-a-tat-tat* followed by a distant shrill scream knifed through her, leaving an icy lump in her stomach.

"Don't you hear that?" she hissed at Jamie, who'd gripped her upper arm as she half-turned toward the increasing commotion behind them.

But Jamie was oblivious to everything except his long-tamped frustration. "Enough, Olivia! It's been six months since the trial. Six months with you obsessing over lessons with that washed-up karate teacher old enough to be your father. And you've been decidedly uninterested in me. Are you sleeping with him?"

"What?" asked Olivia, temporarily distracted from whatever was happening around them to focus on her boyfriend.

Time stopped.

In that moment, Olivia took in Jamie's angry, accusatory expression, the scruffy, unshaven cheeks, and the over-long hair waving across his forehead and curling around his ears. He smelled like sugary alcohol and sweat. She saw with a clarity she rarely had before. It was as if the background behind Jamie had blurred, throwing him in stark relief.

"Are you really this self-absorbed?" she asked.

A heartbeat later she saw them: heavily bearded men moving in parallel across the beach, calmly shooting at the suddenly screaming beachgoers who ran in all directions like water droplets on a hot skillet. Bodies dropped, splayed, their sightless eyes staring at the tumult. Many headed toward the sea only to be caught between the serene blue saltwater and two men picking them off.

Like fish in a barrel, thought Olivia.

Jamie started to answer her question, caught himself when Olivia flinched, and looked over his shoulder.

"Holy shit!" he yelled and, grabbing at her arm, pulled her toward the trees lining the beach.

Olivia stumbled along after him as ice water flooded her veins.

The sun flared overhead. Then the medal branded her like a magnifying glass aimed at an ant. It melted the numbness that had weighted Olivia's feet. She dug her heels into the shifting sand.

Keep your cool, her *sensei*'s voice reminded her. *Running away from a fight doesn't mean uncontrolled flight. You don't want to go from the frying pan into the fryer, got me?*

"What're you doing?" yelled Jamie as her arm slipped from his grasp.

Ignoring him, Olivia pivoted and rapidly counted the number of men with automatic weapons.

Four. Four fucking terrorists.

Not so different from Jin, just killing from a distance. At least he'd used his hands on Emily's throat. Hands and rope.

No uncontrolled anger, either. The derision in her *sensei*'s voice cleared Olivia's thoughts.

She looked at Jamie, so pale with fear he almost glowed. "Taking a beat so we don't run into something worse."

Jamie's gaze turned wild. "That goddamn *sensei* of yours. He'll get you killed." He reached for her. "You're coming with me. Now."

A shadow loomed in the trees behind Jamie. Olivia gripped his forearm and sank her weight into her heels at the same time, tugging hard.

A moment later a bearded man with dead eyes like the victims bleeding out in the sand lunged toward her boyfriend. Olivia caught the sight of something black and pointed in his fist, but she'd already pulled Jamie toward her, stepping to the side as he lurched headlong into the ground.

Knife, her gut shrieked, but her brain slowed down.

She'd run through self-defense drills just last week on how to handle an attacker wielding a knife.

You're going to get cut, her *sensei* reminded her. *You can't avoid it.*

The attacker stopped a meter short of them, his eyes focusing briefly on Olivia, who stood still, both hands up in front of her face, her fingers and wrists loose.

Her peripheral vision caught Jamie coming to his knees. Her boyfriend's lips moved, but she heard nothing except the sounds of the attacker's movements, which were preternaturally loud.

The attacker smiled. It was pure evil. Then he rushed at her, the knife slashing.

Olivia sidestepped and grabbed his shirt, turning as she pushed. The attacker staggered a few steps. Jamie threw himself out of the way.

The attacker caught his balance and swung toward Olivia, who'd backed away and planted her feet in a ready stance. His mouth widened in a nasty sneer. The gaze wasn't so dead now.

"*Putain.*" *Whore.* He spat the curse. In French.

Olivia responded in kind. "*Va te faire enculé, connard.*" *Go fuck yourself, asshole.*

Rage practically lit his gaze red. Olivia's own emotions shut down. Icy calm filled her. He was going to kill her, but she'd make this asshole bleed first.

"Run," she said to Jamie, who'd gotten to his feet.

He ran.

A second after she'd yelled, the attacker lunged. Olivia blocked his knife hand with a forearm, stepping inside his reach to meet him. The knife sliced through her skin, but Olivia scarcely felt it as she punched the heel of her free hand up into his jaw. The attacker's head snapped back. Olivia followed her punch with an elbow strike to the man's face as it came back down. His knees buckled. He crumpled to the ground.

He did not, however, drop the knife. As Olivia danced back from him, he jerked the knife up, catching Olivia's flank. The razor-sharp tip plunged into her side.

She felt *that*.

Instead of fear, however, fury ignited inside her. Planting her feet, she sent a low roundhouse kick into the attacker's head, relishing the satisfying *thud* as it connected. He dropped like a boulder to the side. The impact jarred her all the way into her hip, the knife wound still only a minor sting.

Good came her *sensei*'s voice. *You didn't break your foot at least. Now reset.*

Olivia backed up, her hands up in front of her face again, ready for another assault. Blood slicked the side of her swimsuit, steaming in the sun.

The man didn't move, however. Her foot had connected with his temple. He was either out cold or dead.

She hoped dead.

Darting forward, she bent and pried the knife—which looked like nothing she'd ever seen before—from the attacker's limp fingers. Then she backpedaled, holding the knife in her dominant right hand with both hands again in front of her face.

Only to find herself confronted by a bearded man holding a weapon across his body who watched her with an intensity that sent a bolt of insanity-inducing dread through her. He raised the weapon and aimed at her.

Olivia sucked in a breath, the instinct to run overwhelming. Instead she threw up a wild, spontaneous prayer.

Please let the bastard be out of bullets.

Which was immediately followed by the clicking sound of an empty cartridge as he engaged the trigger—and then repeated the futile gesture.

Stunned disbelief transformed the monster's visage. Olivia chose the better part of valor and, turning, sprinted toward the trees lining the beach where Jamie had disappeared what seemed like eons ago but was in all likelihood only thirty seconds before.

A rough growl followed by the sound of a something hitting the sand came to Olivia's ears. Other chaotic sounds, grunts and gunfire, and a few screams competed with the harsh breathing of the gunman as he neared her. She didn't dare look back or around but put her face down and sped toward the trees, certain that if she could just get a little distance between her and the enraged madman behind her that she could get away....

A heavy hand clamped onto her shoulder and jerked her around. Olivia lost her footing and teetered, unbalanced. As she threw her arm out to catch herself, she realized that she still held the wicked-looking obsidian knife.

She jabbed it at her attacker just as he slammed an iron fist into her face, sending her head back so hard she felt a crunch in her neck. Stars burst in her vision, leaving a fuzzy afterglow.

Panic nearly took rein of her thoughts.

Breathe, Olivia, said her *sensei* in her ear as if he stood next to her in the *dojo. Strike.*

Olivia followed the disembodied voice's command and punched the knife into the attacker's torso. Somewhere in the back of her mind she noted how it felt, the absolute horror of the blade sinking into living flesh, how hot blood gushed over her hand, making the knife handle slippery.

But neither she nor the bearded man stopped in their life-and-death struggle. He hit her again. She gripped the knife harder and stabbed again. And again.

Even as the attacker wrapped steel fingers around her throat and squeezed, Olivia flailed with the knife, no longer stabbing but slicing across whatever body part she could touch with the blade's keen edge.

Bleed, asshole, she thought as darkness edged her vision and a rushing sound filled her ears.

Then they were falling, hard, to the gritty sand as blackness suffocated Olivia.

Sam Ahren knelt, resting his weapon on the ground within easy reach, and shoved the dead terrorist off the young blonde before reaching over and checking her neck for a pulse. There was one, weak, but definitely a flutter. He scanned her for obvious mortal injury. A massive blood stain soaked the left side of her modest two-piece swimsuit. Her battered face had already started to swell, and the bastard had left massive fingerprints on her slender neck.

Sweet Jesus, but it was a miracle she was still alive.

A ray of sunlight glinted on the small metallic disc on her chest. Sam lifted it. A St. Michael's medal. He raised his hand to his own medal, tucked inside his shirt.

As his men moved around the bodies on the beach, checking for survivors, Sam slid the tank top on the young woman up. Knife wound, not bullet. Probably from the combat knife she still gripped in her right hand.

Sam shook his head, disbelief struggling with the evidence in front of him. He glanced over his shoulder at the other dead terrorist five or six meters away.

This young woman, who could be his daughter for Chrissake, that's how old she was, had not only disarmed one of the bastards but engaged hand-to-hand with another one. She'd slashed him into ribbons. Hell, most of the blood on her came from the evil prick. If Sam hadn't shot him, the terrorist would likely have collapsed halfway to the street.

He'd weeded out less successful Rangers from his team. If she lived, he wanted to find out just exactly how an American college student, if he had to guess her nationality and occupation, had managed to survive the terrorist attack that had just killed dozens of other young partyers.

"Demon Pup!" he called to Jess, the team medic, who'd just stood up after checking a body. "Got a warm one here, but she's lost a lot of blood."

Jess double-timed it to them, dropping to his knees next to the young woman. The former corpsman's linebacker size made her appear even more fragile. But that was a deadly illusion. Sam's gut told him that this fierce warrior still wouldn't cower even if threatened by a massive bully. Generally, not the best idea, but if she read people as well as she'd read the preceding assault, she'd probably intuit that the 'demon pup' medic had his warm and fuzzy side, one that wouldn't allow him to hurt an innocent woman.

One strapped with a suicide vest was another matter, however. Jess would put *her* down like a rabid dog in a heartbeat.

"How has she not stopped breathing?" asked Jess after giving the blonde a cursory check. "And what possessed her to tangle with these dickheads?"

He said this without looking up, instead moving his hands quickly and efficiently through the battlefield medicine routine necessary to stabilize someone gravely wounded. Then he ripped open a pouch of QuikClot combat gauze, the DOD's new wonder bandage for stopping blood loss in the field, and smoothed it over the young woman's gut wound. Average Joes in the sandbox had yet to gain access to this newfangled hemostatic dressing, but the foolhardy tourist here in Ibiza now had a much better chance of living thanks to the Special Activites Division's early-access procurement program.

Sam swallowed some water. Tepid though it was, it eased his parched throat. Then he responded to Jess's observation. "Whatever it was, it was the right thing to do in this case. She took out two of those bastards and survived long enough for you to patch her up, doc."

Jess inserted an IV needle before looking up at Sam.

"*You* shot that one," he said, gesturing with his chin at the dead terrorist that Sam had rolled off the college student.

Sam shrugged. "He was expectant. I just moved him along to his final paradise. *She* gets all the credit in my playbook." He turned to Nick, another team member, who'd jogged up to deliver a situation report. "Hey, Playdough, what's the word?"

Nick, his face shiny with sweat behind his dark, reflective sunglasses, kept scanning the beach even as he responded. He wouldn't stand down until after the local first responders appeared.

"Six Red Zebs, all dead," the former Army weapons sergeant said of the terrorists.

Sam's group referred to all terrorists using Arabic slang for *dick*; *red* signaled their status as unlawful enemy combatants. Sometimes the team called them *yooks*, having turned the odious acronym UEC into an ugly word. The team often joked after neutralizing terrorists that they'd taken down *redshirt yooks*, a reference to the irrelevant crew members on Star Trek who often got killed on away missions.

These particular terrorists were members of the Moroccan *Salafia Jihadia*, whom they'd had under magnifying glass for the past six months.

Nick paused in his surveillance to take a swig from his canteen before adding, "Twenty-eight casualties, two survivors including your girl here. Everyone else escaped to the surrounding streets. Won't know 'til later how many report to the local ER with gunshot or stab wounds. Sidewinder and Sleepy Boy have doubled back to look for the *yooks'* staging point."

Sam nodded. The outcome was about what he expected. If only they'd gotten here sooner.... "Goes without saying we recover everything useful before local LE."

Nick nodded. "Roger that, Uncle."

Their intel had the cell hitting the ferry terminal tomorrow morning as the ferries dropped off their daily Spanish visitors. It was sheer dumb luck—*or a miracle*, his brain whispered—that Sleepy Boy had spotted one of the terrorists from their mission brief while at a local market this morning and followed him. Even though they'd scrambled on a dime, they'd lost five minutes to the terrorists. Five minutes meant dozens dead.

In the distance, the shrill sound of sirens pierced the oppressive afternoon air.

Jess looked up at them. "I've done all I can to stabilize her. Time to move. We can't wait for the local ambulance to get here."

"We'll take the truck," said Sam, referring to one of two vehicles the team had acquired for this operation. When Jess looked at him in surprise, he added. "I'm riding along for this one. Playdough, you've got operational control. Make like ghosts before the locals get here."

At Sam's command, Nick faded into the trees, heading to his teammates Evan and Blaylock, codenamed Sidewinder and Sleepy Boy respectively.

A minute later, he and Jess lifted the young woman on a collapsible stretcher that the medic always carried in his backpack. Jess held the front handles and had just started off at a trot with Sam keeping pace when the young woman opened her haunting blue-gray eyes and looked at him.

TWO

Muffled male voices gradually penetrated the thick darkness enveloping Olivia, who rocked on an ocean of fiery pain. Slowly the ocean receded a little, drying her mouth and choking her throat with cotton. Dull pain settled in a tidal pool in her abdomen. She struggled to open her heavy lids, which wouldn't obey her.

That made her angry. She *needed* to see her fate. Her lids snapped wide.

Now Olivia stared from a reclined position at a tall, middle-aged man more fit than most of the male college students she knew back at Brown. He wore a harsh commanding expression, but when his gaze connected with hers, it softened. A little.

Then he looked past her to someone else. "Doc, your patient isn't exactly out."

This was followed by some colorful—and unfamiliar—profanity. Despite that, the tall man and his unseen partner set Olivia down gently. And then after 'Doc' rummaged around out of sight, nimble fingers took her hand, where she realized an IV needle had been taped. Almost immediately, the darkness blotted out the sun and her pain.

The next time she became conscious, a loud rumbling roar filled her ears, and her body, almost weightless, rocked and jostled.

A school bus?

That seemed like a stupid thought, but her mind wouldn't focus, and she didn't have any energy at all for cleansing anger or jolting fear. She couldn't lift her eyelids, though she did move her fingers against something scratchy that covered her. A massive headache waited in the far reaches of her brain....

She heard a slight moan. Hers?

"Your girl has the metabolism of a horse" came an unfamiliar voice, shouting over the roar. "Only Sleepy Boy needs as much sedative."

"A thoroughbred, if that's the analogy we're going with," yelled the voice of the tall man whose face was the last thing she'd seen ... where? "Just knock her out, Doc."

Someone lifted her hand, and peaceful quiet descended.

When consciousness returned to Olivia again, the headache that had loomed now pounded at the door to her head. The tidal pool of pain in her abdomen had evaporated into a dense, hot mass that throbbed as soon as she focused on it. Heavy magnets pulled her eyelids closed. Dizzy, she strained to open them. She laid on something cushioned, and cool cloth draped over her. Even without opening her eyes, she sensed a room around her. Then the electrical hum of equipment wove its way into her exhaustion.

"Stop fighting the sedative," said an irritated male voice.

The tall man. The one her unconscious mind had dubbed 'Commander.' There was something about him. He reminded her of *Sensei*

Mark somehow. So she obeyed, floating away on the powerful drug's cool, dark waters.

The next time Olivia awoke, it was the waking from natural sleep instead of a drugged one. She kept her eyes closed, however, and listened to the sounds in the room around her.

Because she was definitely in a room and not swaying on the ocean or bouncing on a school bus. Somehow she knew that it was a hospital room.

Duh, Olivia, she thought. *You were stabbed, sedated, and carried from the scene of the attack.*

Attack. Terrorists had gunned down everyone around her on the beach in Sant Antoni. A tourist's paradise, someplace she'd run to as an escape from the anguish and anger surrounding Emily's murder.

She inhaled sharply as her memory transported her back to the mayhem, people falling with a peculiar thud, blood splattering and soaking the white sands, screams of terror that were cut short by staccato gunfire. The charcoal and sulfur scent of gunpowder mixed with the coppery scent of blood and the mineral scent of the bay.

Sudden nausea gripped Olivia at the vivid sense information flooding her that she'd ignored at the time. She managed to roll over before vomiting over the side of her bed.

Someone hustled to her side, brushing hair from her face and placing a heavy, warm palm on her upper back. The spasms wracking her eased at the touch.

"Easy there," said the Commander as he helped her to return to the bed.

Olivia stared at the stranger as he pushed a button on the wall behind her. He was tall and muscular just as she recalled from her brief glimpse at the beach. Something about his posture belied the scruffy haircut and stubble. He not only reminded her of her *sensei*, something told her that he used to wear a military uniform.

He turned to her. His tanned skin and the gray streaking his dark hair added health and gravitas to an otherwise unkempt appearance. Somehow she suspected that the Commander would always look commanding.

The stranger studied her. Olivia waited. Almost two years of biting her tongue and biding her time during Jin's murder trial had taught her many things, not the least of which was that waiting to speak often gave the listener power in the conversation, most especially over oneself. And it kept information from the other person. Oh, it also provided the listener with non-verbal information, which was useful, too, and gave one the ability to evaluate surroundings as well as whatever words came out of the speaker's mouth.

Though she would have been wiser to speak up sooner to her aunt and uncle about Jin.

The stranger narrowed his penetrating gray eyes. Olivia had the odd idea that he knew exactly what she was doing and was a little annoyed. And maybe a little impressed, too. She was too exhausted and wary to allow herself even the hint of a smile at that thought, however.

A moment into their staring contest and a burly male wearing scrubs bustled in with a plastic bucket and headed toward the side of the bed where Olivia had thrown up. Neither the Commander nor Olivia spoke while the orderly cleaned up the mess. Olivia noticed that he had a buzzcut. The Commander followed the orderly into the hall where Olivia caught the murmur of speech. In German.

Interesting.

She focused on the almost-inaudible conversation that followed, finding that if she did so that she caught most of the words. By the time the Commander returned, she knew he had told the orderly to bring her food and to send someone to help her use the toilet.

That, too, was interesting. What disheveled outsider in scrubby khakis directed a hospital employee in his duties toward a patient? And where was she for God's sake?

The Commander returned to her bedside, folding an arm at his waist and bringing the other hand to his chin as he studied her. That's when Olivia noticed the chair next to her bed. Sudden insight told her that the Commander had waited—perhaps slept—in that chair while she was unconscious. What did *that* mean?

"I can see by the wheels turning in your head that you're trying to figure out who I am and where you are," said the Commander. His rough baritone matched the stubble on his cheeks. He looked tired. "Which, on the one hand, means you're in charge of your wits. Congratulations for that, by the way. Not every young woman in a swimsuit stabbed by a terrorist on the beach wakes up wary of the man who saved her, but that's the smart play."

Olivia heard a thread of frustration, and maybe anger, in his voice.

"But then again, you're not every young woman, are you Olivia Markham?"

That got Olivia's attention. She sat upright, pulling on the bandage and, presumably, stitches in her side. She winced. The Commander just watched her.

Now who had the power in the conversation?

"How do you know my name?" she asked, unable to control the wariness that colored her tone. Did she have to sound so damn young?

You are *young,* an inner voice chided her.

Don't let your youth hold you back, her *sensei's* voice responded. Use it to your advantage. *Everyone will underestimate you. The foolish will underestimate you because you are a woman.*

Olivia raised her chin and lifted her chest a little. She held the Commander's gaze.

"I know all about you because of what I'm about to tell you, which is classified."

"Then don't tell me," said Olivia, cutting him off.

The Commander, about to speak, stopped short and blinked several times.

"Obviously you're some sort of soldier, like on that TV show. The Unit. You're like Jonas, the master sergeant." Olivia caught the startled looked in the stranger's eyes. "Are you Delta Force? Are we at an Army base in Germany?"

Before he could answer her questions, the door to her room opened. Instead of the orderly, it was another man. This clean-shaven stranger with iron-gray hair wore a dark, expensive-looking suit. And a hard expression. Fine grooves bracketed his compressed lips.

"How in the world did she take control of the conversation?" he asked the Commander in German without looking at her. "She's a friggin' sophomore in college, for Chrissake! I know you have a hard-on for her, but get a grip, Uncle, she's half your age and out of your league. Don't play the fool over her."

Oh, no, he didn't just talk about her *in front of* her.

"Who are you?" she demanded. In German. And just to drive her point home, she said, "And where is that tray of food 'Uncle' ordered? I'd also like to wash my face and hair and brush my teeth."

The newcomer whipped his gaze to hers. The Commander gave a slow, wide smile that warmed Olivia's heart.

"I'll just go see about it," he said, humor twinkling for a moment in his gaze. "I think the orderly may have been sidetracked"—here his gaze slipped to the side for the fraction of an instant, inadvertently signaling to Olivia that it was at the newcomer's order—"and I think you've got this situation under control, Yesterday."

Yesterday? As in "like yesterday"? Was that sarcasm? Directed at her? Or the new guy, who seemed like the Commander's superior?

The newcomer watched the other man leave before he turned back to Olivia. "You speak German as well as French. There are reports of you swearing at one of the terrorists."

Olivia ignored his implied question to ask, "Jamie? He's alive then?"

The man in front of her tilted his head, studying her. "You're a rare one, Ms. Markham, aren't you?" he asked, but it was clearly rhetorical. "Uncle didn't oversell you."

Olivia had had enough of this indirection and, frankly, lack of courtesy for someone gravely injured by a terrorist.

"Where am I, Yesterday?" She paused and held his gaze, firming her chin and imagining that she gripped her favorite martial arts weapon, a *bō* staff. *Sensei* Mark said she had a particular affinity for it. She imagined the sound the *bō* would make knocking upside this jerk's head.

He recoiled as if she had hit him with the fantasy weapon.

"You, Ms. Markham," he said in an acerbic tone, "are in a CIA facility in Germany, as you correctly identified."

"Near Mannheim," said Olivia before asking, "What about Jamie?"

Yesterday looked thunderstruck, and then his brows lowered. "James Stone wasn't injured in the Ibiza attack. He's already back in the States, reunited with his family." He enunciated each word slowly and clearly, his pale eyes growing frostier if possible. "Tell me, Ms. Markham, how do you know that we're near Mannheim?"

Olivia shrugged. She could share this little tidbit. It gave very little away, except perhaps that she might understand more than French and German. "I sang in choir in high school. We toured Europe a couple of times. I just noticed the difference between the way we pronounced German words and how the local speakers pronounced them. For instance, you sound like you learned your German in Berlin."

At that moment the Commander returned, bringing a paper cup with a lid and straw. He set it on the side table next to Olivia.

"Someone will bring you food and toiletries after Yesterday leaves," he said to her.

Irritation winged across Yesterday's features, but he schooled them into an impassive display so quickly that Olivia might not have seen it if she hadn't been looking.

But she had. Experience had taught her to keep the predator always in view. She doubted that he would take it out on the Commander, but he'd try to take it out on her if he got the opportunity. People like Yesterday always needed to feel superior to anyone they viewed as weak and vulnerable. And beautiful young women were tasty prey to them.

Just not *her*. If he tried to take a bite out of her, he'd find that she had a nasty aftertaste.

Though that was bravado speaking. There wasn't much she could do, injured and in Germany with two men she didn't know. She darted a glance at the Commander. She may not know him, but her gut told her that she could trust him.

Both men stepped back from her bed, the Commander taking a stance at the foot, his arms crossed at his waist. Yesterday remained a few steps closer and to the side.

He began speaking again. "Ms. Markham, you have a remarkable set of gifts."

"You mean, for a woman?" she asked, cutting him off. She didn't like him, and the only way to keep him from having all the power in the conversation was to prevent him from controlling it.

"I mean for anyone, your age or older," he said in a sharp tone. "Now, let me speak. You listen—"

"No."

"What?" Fury flattened Yesterday's already tight mouth.

"Whatever you have to say to me can wait until I use the toilet and brush my teeth. Or you're just another terrorist with a suit and tie." She bared her teeth. "And I don't give in to terrorists."

She said the second part in Mandarin. She didn't care if he didn't understand the words. He clearly understood her meaning.

Yesterday nodded once. "All right, then. We'll give you fifteen minutes to take care of your human needs."

He glanced over at the Commander, who followed the suited officer to the door. There, the Commander looked back at Olivia and did something unexpected. He winked.

Olivia sank back against her pillow as the door closed. Good grief, but she was tired. And she hurt. Besides that, her mouth still felt like the inside of an Easy Bake oven: hot and dry. She forced herself to drink down the water in the paper cup that the Commander had left before attempting to get out of the bed, which had rails.

Fifteen minutes? Did Yesterday really say fifteen minutes? It had seemed like plenty of time when he said it.

Olivia had managed to get the rail to fold down and had swung her legs to the side when a soft knock preceded the door opening, followed by a woman's head peeking around its edge.

"Would you like some help?" she asked in accented English.

"Yes, thank you," said Olivia. It was always a good idea to be polite at the outset, but decisive. It was something her mother had instilled in her very young.

It took the remainder of the time that she'd negotiated to make it to the small bathroom next to her room, empty her bladder, and brush her teeth. And she wouldn't even have managed to do that without Marta's help. But the other woman told her in a cheerful voice that she'd happily shove Yesterday's head in the toilet after Olivia finished, if that's what it took to get Olivia back into bed before the odious man returned.

Olivia laughed, then regretted it, and laughed again as Marta helped her into the bed. And not a moment too soon because Yesterday and the Commander came in as Marta raised the rail.

"You can bring her food tray in after we leave," said Yesterday without looking at the nurse.

"Where is she from?" asked the Commander after the door closed behind Marta.

"You mean Marta?" asked Olivia. Neither man reacted, but she knew from a slight change in their posture that she'd gotten their attention for some reason. She narrowed her eyes in thought. "I don't know."

A gleam lit Yesterday's eyes. "Really?"

The Commander tilted forward slightly as if encouraging Olivia to reconsider her answer.

Olivia shrugged the shoulder on her good side. "It's obviously Bavarian, but there's a trace of something else in her speech ... I don't think she's originally from Germany."

The Commander smiled. Yesterday remained focused.

"Very impressive, Ms. Markham. German to a fine degree, French, Mandarin—it was Mandarin, wasn't it? Isn't that the language that your cousin Emily's killer spoke at home?—" he kept speaking over her startled gasp—"any other languages that I should know about?"

Should know about. Ha! As if she were in some sort of trouble, rather than an interesting specimen to him.

Olivia ignored the question. She wouldn't tell this one any more. He clearly knew more than enough already.

"Have you notified my parents about my injury? What have you told them about where I'm at? When can I leave?"

She shot-gunned the questions at the older CIA officer. In her limited experience, adults her parents' age got uncomfortable by the childish tactic. They still hadn't quite figured out how to interact with her.

Not Yesterday. He clearly couldn't give a shit what she tried to do.

"We'll get back to your questions," he said.

The Commander shifted at the end of the bed and crossed his hands in front of him. Olivia glanced at his inscrutable expression.

Yesterday continued. "For now, suffice it to say that you were correct when you guessed that Uncle here commands a special operations team at the Agency's behest, but that's as far as I'm prepared to go in sharing details with you."

Olivia didn't interrupt, simply nodding at his statement. Her curiosity burned, however.

"I procure ... things ... for the CIA's Special Operations Group. Mostly that means weapons, vehicles, gear. But my position has a certain latitude, shall we say, for recruiting exceptional individuals into SOG. Uncle's description of your actions on the beach in Ibiza as well as my own observations today confirm that you're an individual of interest for a future operation."

Whatever Olivia thought Yesterday was going to say, *that* wasn't it.

"I don't understand," she said, looking at the Commander for any clue to deciphering Yesterday's statement. She discerned none on the older man's face. "You just said, and I quote, 'she's a friggin' college sophomore.' What can I do for the CIA?"

"Ms. Markham, the War on Terror has hardly even begun. What happened in Ibiza is just the most obvious and regrettable action in that war. Rather, there are a thousand and one things that lead up to that moment when a group of armed *jihadis* stroll through a busy tourist area, gunning down infidel women in bikinis. Most of it involves money, and powerful people, especially powerful men, with money."

"And that's where I come in?" asked Olivia. A hint of bitterness crept into her voice despite her best efforts to sound neutral.

Yesterday nodded. His gaze had honed into that of a predator, watching her so intently that warning coursed down her spine. "Powerful men bent on sponsoring terror wall themselves off from direct threats and conduct business with suspicion and care."

"But when it comes to a beautiful woman, they think with the wrong head," said the Commander.

Olivia shot him an outraged glare. "So you want to dangle me as bait."

"No,' said Yesterday, shaking his head. "We want to recruit and train you to get close to Chase Graham, the scion of the founder of Graham Investments."

"The private equity firm? Isn't Chase Graham one of the most eligible bachelors in the world according to the tabloids? What's he got to do with the War on Terror?"

Now Yesterday looked grim. "We believe he's a major contributor to terrorism."

THREE

Five days later, the eight-hour Lufthansa flight back to Boston took at least seven hours too long in Olivia's estimation. A taciturn man wearing sunglasses and nondescript clothing had met her at the CIA facility at five a.m. and escorted her to the waiting, equally nondescript, black sedan outside. He handed her a small bag containing her personal effects from Ibiza, including her passport, which she'd left locked in the hotel safe. She'd already gotten her suitcase delivered the day before with all of her clothes washed and neatly folded inside.

Then he drove her in silence to the airport where he showed some credentials at the airport security office and left her with another taciturn escort, this time a sour-looking blonde who resisted Olivia's efforts at polite chitchat. The blonde bypassed the security queue and drove Olivia in a scooter directly to her gate, where she was boarded before the other passengers.

She was exhausted and stiff long before she got on the jet. Her wound had healed enough that the German doctor who released her had been satisfied that she could manage on painkillers and antibiotics until she got home and found a local surgeon for follow-up care.

At least the CIA had sprung for a business-class seat where the attendant brought her juice and coffee even before the flight took off. She'd never flown in such large, comfortable seats and was grateful for the small mercy. Idly she wondered how field officers traveled. Probably in coach, if the nondescript black sedan was anything to go by.

Of course, that spurred thoughts of Larry Starling, the CIA paramilitary operations officer otherwise known as Yesterday. He and Sam Ahren, whose code name Uncle made more sense once she learned his real name, had spent several visits explaining as much about the operation involving Chase Graham and her proposed role in targeting him that they could without revealing classified information. For Olivia, it was enough to know that a handsome, wealthy celebrity bachelor who made the covers of all the supermarket tabloids *and* popped up on Reddit and Tumblr and the dying MySpace failed to live up to the fairytale image.

Yesterday pulled no punches, though, when he warned her that no one would believe her if she tried to suggest publicly that Graham was a person of interest.

"But it will alert him that we're looking into his activities, so I would prefer it if you don't broadcast the news," he said.

Olivia understood. "It sounds like a lose-lose proposition," she said.

Too bad she couldn't tell her mother about Graham. He was attractive and wealthy enough to have made his way into her mother's Facebook and Twitter feeds.

Sam had smiled at her answer, which she realized on the flight home meant that she'd passed some sort of test.

It explained why Yesterday had shared the target's name.

Target.

It was the same word that archers used.

Archers and shooters.

A large round archery target wavered in her memory as she looked out the Lufthansa jet window. She'd enjoyed archery over years of summer camp and had been good enough to compete at the national level in high school. She'd even qualified for the Olympic team. Brown University, however, didn't have a competitive team, and she'd chosen to abandon archery in favor of plans for medical school. And then after Emily died, she'd joined the Shotokan Karate Club at Brown.

But maybe her years of target practice could be put to use with a handgun or rifle....

Her neck tingled. The St. Michael medal seemed to warm in a kind of warning.

Olivia shook her head. What in the hell was she thinking?

Obviously about the attack. She'd started having nightmares once they'd stopped sedating her, and a pervasive sense of unease shadowed her even here on the jet. True, the 9-11 attacks had been conducted with commandeered jets, but airport security had tightened almost unbearably for ordinary travelers.

Unless you bypassed the system entirely, as she'd done. How likely was that to happen twice on the same flight? And if it did, didn't it suggest that the passenger had been vetted beforehand?

She refrained from looking around for the male passenger who'd caught her attention as he boarded, but once she'd let the memory of holding a recurve bow go, she found that she fixated on him.

It didn't make sense. He seemed quite ordinary, with dark-brown hair, designer glasses, a striped polo shirt and gray casual pants, and some sort of tan European walking shoe. He carried a worn black leather messenger bag that she'd seen a lot of in Germany. He read as an architect or tech developer of some sort, stylish without being too cutting edge.

Nevertheless, she felt his gaze on her even though she only managed to catch him looking at her once, when she abruptly stood to get her bag from the overhead bin. As she skimmed her gaze over him as she rose, she'd seen the intent way that he watched her. It creeped her out. Even before Ibiza, she'd been extra sensitive to the attention that she drew from others, men and women. Most of it was benign, but occasionally she caught a glimpse of something darker. Malevolent.

The plane landed a couple of hours later, and the German passenger—she'd heard him saying *thank you* to the Lufthansa flight attendant in German—disappeared in the crowd spewing from the gate into the concourse. Olivia dawdled and took her time in the women's restroom so that when she exited, the concourse had cleared out. The German passenger had disappeared. At the customs kiosks, Olivia presumed that her admirer had been swallowed in the mass of arriving travelers, which included her. Or had lawfully skirted the uniformed officials. Either way, he was no longer a threat to her over-strung nerves.

Her parents met her outside security. Olivia had never been so glad or so relieved to see their faces. They waited patiently for her to come to them, giving Olivia time to note the extra fine lines around her mother's eyes and mouth that deepened as she smiled at her eldest daughter. Her father's hair, already salt-and-pepper, had lost more of the pepper, but otherwise he looked tan and fit as he always did, and his smile was as broad and warm.

Olivia opened both arms, and they surrounded her.

She inhaled deeply, imbibing her mother's perfume, an elegant, classic floral scent of gardenia, jasmine, and tuberose. Tears pricked her eyes at the familiar, warm scent, but she swallowed and hugged her parents as hard as she could, even though it tugged on her stitches.

Her father stepped back while her mother placed a palm on Olivia's cheek and studied her intently. Olivia knew that nothing got past her mother, but she also knew that her mother wouldn't pressure her for details.

Instead, her mother pulled her into a tight embrace, kissing her cheek and saying in a thick voice, "You look like you've been through hell, but better than I feared. I'm so happy that you're home and safe. I'm not sure I'll want to let you out of my sight now."

Olivia's father smiled. "I have no problem with you going anywhere and doing anything, anytime. Jamie's been telling everyone that you saved his life. I knew you were fierce, little girl, just not *that* fierce."

Olivia laughed, the tears drying.

Her parents had always treated their children as capable of handling whatever life threw at them, though Olivia knew that they'd tried to balance how quickly she and her brother and sister would be asked to shoulder responsibility.

Unfortunately, facing the murder of someone you love wasn't one of the things that they could have shielded their children from. In their own way, they were as lost as Olivia in how to handle the grief. But they got up every day, got dressed, and went about the business of living. Olivia supposed that even in this they did what they could for their children.

"I'm starving. Can we get a burger and fries on the way home?" she asked as they headed toward baggage to claim her suitcase.

As they did, she glimpsed the German traveler heading out the airport doors toward ground transportation. He pulled a small suitcase and never looked her way. A weight that she hadn't realized pressed on her shoulders lifted. In eight short hours, that German had come to represent all of the troubling past two weeks, and she shoved him and the memory of that time into a locked closet in the back of her mind.

Olivia spent the next week settling back into her routine at home, though once the pain and swelling subsided in her abdomen, she found her limitations clashing with her returning energy. She missed *Sensei* Mark, and she missed training in the dojo.

But she'd taken the summer off from karate even before getting stabbed. After the Ibiza trip, she'd scheduled a month-long EMT course. It wasn't a clinical rotation by any stretch of the imagination, but she wanted to get into hands-on medical training sooner rather than later. Becoming an EMT was the fastest way to do that as a college student. The young EMT she interviewed on campus last year said that he'd seen some pretty complicated cases involving Brown students, including a collapsed lung after a car crash, a gunshot wound, broken bones, and the inevitable alcohol and drug overdoses.

Jamie came to visit a few days after Olivia returned to Marlborough, a small city about half an hour outside of Boston where she'd grown up. It wasn't the first time that he'd made the trip from Stamford, Connecticut since they'd started dating.

It was weird.

Everything about it, especially how it ended.

She couldn't figure out what to wear, and she wasn't particularly fussy with her appearance. Of course, she'd sometimes put on makeup and blow her hair out when she and Jamie went out on the weekends with friends, but she didn't like the way some guys stared at her even with her boyfriend at her side. And Jamie didn't care anyway. He said she was beautiful without all the extra stuff on her face.

But that mid-June afternoon, they'd both dressed better than they would have before the Ibiza trip, as if it was their first date. And they were still in high school.

Olivia invited Jamie inside, noting his fresh haircut, his uneven shave, and the nice khaki shorts and polo from the upscale mall store. As she closed the door after her boyfriend, she glimpsed a silver Toyota Camry parked down the block on the opposite side of the street, in front of the Paulsens' house.

The Paulsens were in their late seventies and rarely had visitors, except their daughter Lindsey, who lived in the next town over, and her children, who were in high school and college. The man sitting behind the steering wheel had been too old for Tom or Eddie, and Marley didn't date yet. Though it was too far for most people, Olivia had exceptional vision—something her optometrist had commented on, saying she'd make an excellent pilot or sniper.

The driver of the Camry looked an awful lot like the German traveler.

Olivia turned, and Jamie pulled her into his arms before she realized what he intended. Taken off guard, she jerked back.

Jamie flinched. "I'm sorry, Livvy. Did I hurt you?"

"What?" asked Olivia, distracted. "Oh, no, I'm fine. It barely hurts anymore. The doctor can't believe how well I'm healing. She says I'll be able to return to karate in the fall as long as I wait to spar until spring."

She turned toward the family room, reluctant to step back into Jamie's embrace.

"That's good," he said, following her. "Listen." He cleared his throat and began again. "I want to talk about my behavior that day."

Olivia plopped down on the sofa, her thoughts drifting to the man in the Camry. With an effort, she focused on what Jamie was saying. He deserved her attention. Plus, he didn't need to be reminded that she seemed to have extrasensory perception. He was already acting as if she was a stranger, not the young woman he'd dated for the last year, holding her hand when she needed it, letting her cry on his shoulder from time to time but more often gamely acting as a sparring partner, which meant bruises, a sprain, and, once, a broken finger.

She took his hand in hers. "There's nothing to talk about," she said as gently as she could. "I was foolhardy in the extreme. It's a miracle that I survived."

Jamie looked at her, holding her gaze with his honest blue one. She recalled for a heartbeat the way he'd made her feel freshman year. Alive. As she hadn't felt since Emily's brutal murder. She would forever be grateful to him for reminding her that there were still good guys in the world and that she could still feel love and affection.

As soon as Olivia thought this, she knew what was coming.

Jamie squeezed her hand and visibly swallowed. "It's a miracle that *I* survived, Liv. All because of you and your stupid premonitions." He laughed. It was a little shaky. Then he gathered himself, sitting straighter. "I can't face myself in the mirror. I can't sleep, either. I keep seeing—and hearing—all those people...." He swallowed again, and his gaze dropped to their entwined fingers.

"Me too," she said, raising his chin so that he could see that she told the truth. "Jamie, I think we both know why we're so awkward around each other now."

He shrugged. Olivia glimpsed a sheen of tears before he looked away. He cleared his throat again and brought his gaze back to hers. He raised his free hand to stroke her cheek. "I love you, Olivia Markham. I think I always will. You'll be the standard I measure every other woman against."

"Please don't," she whispered, pressing her cheek into his palm. It was her turn to clear her throat. "I'm not worth it. And it wouldn't be fair to the woman you deserve."

He nodded and dropped his hand, standing at the same time. "Tell Michael and Dianne I said hi."

Olivia's brother and sister had grown quite fond of Jamie. They'd probably be more stunned and heartbroken than she was that she and Jamie had just broken up.

"I will," she said.

After she walked Jamie to the front door, she confirmed that the Toyota remained. It was there but empty. Doubtless the German—or CIA officer as she suspected—hadn't expected Jamie to stay such a short time. As she closed the door, Olivia glanced around the front hall, her senses tingling. It almost felt as though someone had just been in here, but no one else was home.

Olivia returned to the family room where a digital piano, site of countless lessons, gave her an excuse to dawdle. And listen.

She sat down and plunked a few keys, but her whole being strained toward the sounds in the house. Her cat Alfred sometimes made a lot of noise when he forgot that he was a rotund ball of fur and kitty chow. But her elderly golden retriever Oliver slept in the sun.

There. A whisper in the hallway above.

Someone was in the house.

Olivia pressed the *play* button on the digital piano. In high school, she'd recorded a sonata she'd composed for her senior recital so that her mother could play it anytime she wanted. As the music began playing, Olivia rose and headed into the living room, where she could return to the front hall without being seen by anyone coming down the stairs. On the way, she grabbed her *bō*, which she'd been practicing forms with before Jamie's arrival.

Sure enough, she reached the doorway in time to see the "German" traveler step from the stairs into the front hall. He didn't even look toward the family room, simply hastened to the front door.

Olivia let the intruder reach it before asking in German, "Doesn't the CIA teach you to wait until the house is empty before going inside?"

The man halted, his gloved fingers on the doorknob. To his credit, he immediately turned and answered in English. "Yesterday said you were some kind of wunderkind, but when you didn't make me at the airport, I figured the old man was finally losing it."

Olivia shrugged but kept her gaze riveted on him. She also kept her stance and grip on the *bō* equally loose and ready to move. "I 'made' you. I just didn't trust my gut. I won't make that mistake again."

"I imagine not." The CIA field officer's gaze dipped to her weapon and then back to her face. "Yesterday clearly underestimates you. You're more than a hip-pocket asset."

The hairs on Olivia's neck stood up. Why did that sound derogatory? "What does that mean?"

It was the field officer's turn to shrug. "Someone he runs on the side, not an official employee. It's easier for him, more deniability, more control. Not so good for you. You don't get real pay or benefits. And no one to appeal to inside the Company."

Olivia smiled. It didn't reach her eyes. "He got a little ahead of himself. I hadn't said I'd work for him yet. Now he's going to have to work harder to recruit me."

"I'll tell him you said so."

"Don't bother. I can speak to him myself."

Humor lit the intruder's gaze. He tilted his head. "I'll leave you to it then." He looked toward the family room. "The piano playing is a nice touch."

After the man left, Olivia went outside. She didn't feel safe in her own home now.

Using her flip phone, she phoned Mark Holberg, her *sensei* and the first person outside of her family that she'd spoken to after returning to the U.S. She couldn't tell her parents that the CIA had come calling after her misguided heroics in Ibiza. They'd likely lose their minds. They definitely would if they knew she was considering accepting Yesterday's pitch.

Sensei Mark had surprised her in that earlier conversation when he'd said, "Let me make a few calls. Some of the guys from my old unit went on to work in the Special Operations Group for the CIA. I'm sure someone knows something about Larry Starling, if that's even his real name."

That possibility had shocked Olivia. She'd sensed no deceit in Yesterday when he'd handed her his business card. Sam Ahren, who seemed more trustworthy, hadn't signaled any discomfort with the act.

Maybe Sam didn't know Starling well....

Fortunately, *Sensei* Mark answered her call almost immediately. The first thing he said when Olivia told him she'd confronted one of Starling's officers in her house was that they needed to meet elsewhere. "In case he planted listening devices. Passive ones won't show up on a sweep."

That really made Olivia's neck tingle. And her ire flare. She agreed.

Forty-five minutes later, they met at the Bellingham mall, about halfway between her house and Providence.

Something about her karate instructor's broad shoulders and shocking blue eyes always put Olivia at ease. She didn't realize how tense she'd been, in fact, until a sigh escaped her as he fell into step at her side.

He handed her a large manila envelope, telling her to put it into her backpack, before strolling next to her through the food court. The surrounding white noise of shoppers, shrieking children, and Musak drowned out all possibility that anyone could overhear them.

"Read that later, your eyes only. For now, I'll give you the short and sweet. Starling is the real deal in terms of procuring people and equipment for SOG ops."

Olivia listened as she slipped the packet into her bag. "So he really does want to use me on a mission. I just don't like what the guy he sent called me: 'a hip-pocket asset.'"

Sensei Mark looked at her, his gaze serious and intent. "What does your gut tell you?"

"That it would be extremely fortunate if there was something in that envelope I can use to get Starling to bring me on as a legitimate CIA employee."

At Olivia's declaration, her karate instructor steered her toward an empty table, pulled out a chair, and pointed. "Sit."

Then he went and bought two sodas.

After he joined her, her mentor wasted no time in getting to the point. "Is that what you want, Olivia, to go into the CIA fulltime?"

"Yes."

She squeezed her eyes shut, remembering the crime-scene photos the detective had shown her. Emily's body in the coffin at the funeral. All those swimsuit-clad tourists on the beach.

Pain lanced through her as real, and visceral, as the combat knife the terrorist had stabbed her with.

Olivia opened her eyes and looked at *Sensei* Mark, who watched her with compassion.

"I want to be trained in a way that I'd never be on my own in your dojo. Working for Starling is the first realistic hope I've had to do that."

"So you can change the course for other innocent people like Emily?" he asked quietly.

She nodded, toying with the straw of her untouched soda.

"Then I think you'll find what you need in there." He tilted his head toward her backpack. "Starling runs ghost assets and pockets the money. But be warned, Olivia. Starling isn't someone you can leverage easily. Keep your wits about you, and leave the evidence someplace secure outside of your parents' house. I'll keep a copy, too, and my buddies will keep an eye out for you when they can."

Olivia nodded again and stood when he did. She had a lot to do, starting with contacting Starling, but she felt better having her mentor's blessing, mixed though it was.

"And Olivia?" When she looked at him, he said, "Your mission and the CIA's won't always match. Be sure you can live with that."

FOUR

Olivia expected to get a phone call from Starling before she returned home, but she didn't hear from him that day or the next. Then it dawned on her that the operative (the term *Sensei* Mark had used) must have taken her at her word and left it to her to make the call to the hard-nosed CIA handler.

She tucked that insight away.

In the future, she'd go with assertive. Events were leading her to understand that that approach was the coin of this new intelligence realm she'd chosen to join. Well, in her case, bravado would have to do because she didn't have much sweat equity, that is, relevant experience, from which to back a bold attitude.

But the more she thought about it, the more she realized that she did have something to leverage beyond the file on Starling that *Sensei* Mark had managed to get for her: herself.

As the good student she was, Olivia had read up on how the Central Intelligence Agency functioned, and she knew that Starling had crossed a line in sending a field officer to surveil an American citizen on U.S. soil, especially one with no ties to any foreign bad actors. The CIA had no mandate to operate within the country, though Olivia suspected that it did anyway.

Starling clearly wanted her badly if he'd risk anyone finding out that he'd broken the law.

Olivia waited until the third day to call Starling. He answered so quickly she wondered if he knew that she was calling. And then she understood that he'd either tapped her cellphone or had her number already in his contacts, probably from the time that it was in the CIA's possession.

"Playing hard to get?" he said without preamble. "Have you had enough time to consider my offer? It's not going to improve with age, by the way."

"Oh, I don't know," she said, forcing cheer into her voice. "Time was all I needed to look into you, Mr. Starling."

He snorted.

"All right," he said, humor clear in *his* voice. "I'll play along. What do you think you've got on me, Ms. Markham?"

"A phone call to the FBI," she said, "who would probably be very interested to learn that—" here she paused as if searching for the information, but she'd memorized the name that the field officer had given the car-rental agency—"Jason Corvid—you must like bird names, Starling—broke into my house *and* planted a tracker on my car. I mean, sure, it would be hard to trace that back to you, but I wouldn't think that you'd like the annoyance of dealing with one of the Boston FBI agents—George Saunders, I think he said his name is—who seemed to take my neighbor, Mrs. Paulsen, very seriously when she called. Probably because he's her son-in-law."

Silence reigned for several long moments in which Olivia sensed Starling seething.

"You're right," he said in an icy tone, "I don't want to deal with the *gnat* that Special Agent Saunders is. But make no mistake, Ms. Markham, he *is* a gnat and nothing more. I don't know what you're maneuvering for, but it's ill-advised in the extreme to threaten me with blackmail."

Despite his tone and words, Starling didn't revoke his earlier pitch for Olivia to work for him to get close to Chase Graham.

Olivia let an inaudible sigh escape. She realized she'd been holding her breath, and her heart tapped like a wounded bird at her ribcage. She counted to five, breathing slowly to get control over her heartrate.

Be able to walk away, Olivia, she heard her *sensei* caution her. She didn't know if he'd actually ever said that to her, but it calmed her nerves to imagine that he had. *If you can't let it go, Starling will use that against you.*

"Then I suppose it's equally ill-advised to tell you that I don't want to be a 'hip-pocket' asset," she said. She kept her voice low to keep it from trembling.

As soon as she said it, she knew that she could walk away.

Starling swore. "That prick Corvid," he said in a way that made it clear he was speaking to himself. "No wonder he missed his check-in." He brought his attention back to her. "You don't have the requirements for me to bring you onboard as a fully vetted asset. You're just a college student, Ms. Markham. You wasted your power play."

Gah. Did people really talk like movie villains in the CIA? *Power play. Right.* He sounded like those stupid bad guys in the thrillers that her dad liked to watch.

Disgust filled Olivia at Starling's terminology.

"Not really," she said, channeling that disgust into a cool voice. "I haven't said anything about becoming an official asset." She paused. "I want to be a legitimate field officer."

Ponderous silence reigned for a full fifteen seconds. Olivia wondered if Starling wanted to make her sweat. She was, but for the love of all that was holy, she would *never* let this man know it. Interacting with him wasn't too different from standing onstage singing a soprano solo at Jordan Hall in Boston.

"That's an interesting possibility," he said at last about her demand. "However, you have to have a college degree followed by eighteen months at The Farm. We can't wait almost four years to put you into the field. It will take months to get you into place with Chase Graham as it is."

That wasn't a direct no. Stubbornness gripped Olivia, filling her with the need to argue. The sweat evaporated. This was her future, for God's sake. And, if it was as dangerous as Starling had said, maybe even her life. She couldn't just go along for the ride and see where it took her.

"That's the standard admissions process," she said. "But I've never been involved in anything that didn't have a fast-track for exceptional cases. I think you can bend the rules a bit for me, Mr. Starling. We can do this in a different order, but I won't work for you unless I'm a legitimate CIA employee."

Starling didn't budge. "I don't have time to handle another *seasoned* paramilitary operations officer from SOG, let alone an untrained field officer from the kiddie pool."

"That's okay. I'd rather have Sam Ahren be my case officer. He was going to train me anyway, right?" Olivia didn't actually know whom

Starling had had in mind to train her, but this at least forced the issue. Might as well hammer out the details here and now.

She heard his harsh sigh through the cellphone speaker.

"Look, I procure gear, weapons, and vehicles overseas. Sometimes that involves recruiting foreign nationals. I have latitude there. But not here in the States as you alluded to earlier. That's why I was going to run you as a hip-pocket asset."

Time to show him that she wouldn't be bullied into something she didn't want.

"Well, then, I'm afraid I can't help you, Mr. Starling. Good luck finding another woman to get close to Chase Graham."

She ended the call.

And then didn't answer the phone when Starling called back. Dating had taught her how to deal with all kinds of male interest. Starling was definitely of the breed of male who likes the thrill of the chase.

In fact, Olivia didn't answer for another three days.

"Mr. Starling," she said before he could do more than say her name when she did, "I thought that I made it clear that I won't work for you as a hip-pocket asset. So unless you're calling me with the news about when I can report to human resources, you need to stop calling me or I'll call George Saunders."

"Listen, Ms. Markham," he said, fairly growling her name. "I don't have time for your fucking nonsense."

"Seems like you do," she interrupted. "I've had dates less persistent than you."

"I want you to know that I spent the last three days assuring that George Saunders is too busy dealing with an internal investigation into his non-existent criminal activities to deal with a request from his mother-in-law's college neighbor."

Olivia's heart sank. She'd never anticipated that throwing George's name around would lead Starling to do something like this.

Sensei Mark had been correct when he said that Starling wouldn't be easy to convince to sponsor her as an official recruit.

"In fact, if you want to continue to play games, I can easily make life hard for you at Brown. Pre-med, are you? That's a very competitive field, I understand. Reputation and clinical hours are almost as important as test scores and classes when applying to med schools."

Well, he'd just escalated that way beyond her threat to turn him into the FBI.

That gave her pause. Did she really want to work with him in any capacity?

Then she remembered that she'd been so focused on navigating this new intelligence world that she'd stopped having nightmares about Emily and the Ibiza terrorist attack.

And Sam Ahren's face wavered to life in her memory. He was a good guy. She was sure of it.

"Well, when you put it that way," she said slowly, "I guess I have no choice."

"No, not really," said Starling. "You've maneuvered yourself into working as my hip-pocket asset."

"That's what I was afraid you'd say." She took a deep breath. It felt like plunging into dark, fathomless water to go on. "Then I'll just have to notify Clarence Gill in the Office of the General Counsel about your ghost assets and the Bahamas bank account associated with them."

"Where did you learn about that?" he asked. "How could you possibly have any evidence?"

Starling sounded like a wounded snake, hissing and genuinely confused.

"Thank you for doing me the honor of not trying to deny it," said Olivia, ignoring the bait about proof.

"Of course not. I should be thanking you instead for alerting me to a vulnerability." Starling's cold voice held a razor edge. "It seems you have the upper hand, Ms. Markham. For now."

Sudden worry for *Sensei* Mark's unnamed friends shot through Olivia. She prayed that they'd be able to take care of themselves. Almost unaware of what she did, she touched the medal hanging between her breasts at the thought. It was warm and reassuring.

"I start EMT training on Monday," she said, returning to her original negotiation plan. "That lasts four weeks. Does that give you enough time to arrange everything?"

"It's adequate."

"It'd better be." She paused a beat before adding, "I'm not upending my life on a plea to make *yours* easier. Send Uncle with employment papers or lose my phone number."

Jerk, she added to herself.

"Copy that," he said.

Afterwards, Olivia, her hands trembling, sat down at her father's desk—she'd hurried to his deserted office to take Starling's call where her siblings couldn't overhear. Her father's lingering presence soothed her nerves.

She'd succeeded.

What had she gotten herself into?

Six weeks later, Olivia found herself on a helicopter piloted by Sam Ahren flying into the mountains of North Carolina to begin training at a private camp. Starling had made good on his part of the bargain, and Olivia was officially a CIA employee, if not technically a recruit.

"You know how it is," Starling said when he called her with the news. "It's easier to promote from inside the organization. This way, I can get you top-secret clearance and nominate you for part-time study at the National Intelligence Defense College in Bethesda. It won't get you out of CIA 101, but it will allow you to earn a bachelor's of science in intelligence before you apply for Clandestine Services. With credentials like those, you'll be at the top of your class at the Farm and able to take more advanced training afterwards."

"What's the catch?" Olivia had asked. "Beyond going part-time while I work on the mission, that is."

"No catch, unless you mean, can you tell anyone what you're doing? And the answer to that is no. The easiest plan for now is for you to announce to your family and friends that you're still traumatized by everything that's happened, and you're taking a leave of absence from school."

"That won't be too hard to sell. My mom's been after me for some time to process what happened to Emily 'in a healthy way.' What do I tell my parents about Bethesda?"

"That's the first test of your covert abilities, Ms. Markham. Most CIA employees either work under an official cover with other federal agencies or under non-official covers. NOCs are day jobs. What 'day job' are you going to take that lets you believably live in Bethesda and be incommunicado for days, possibly weeks?"

Olivia hadn't thought that far ahead. Now, as she sat in the helicopter next to Sam, she ignored the question. She had until the end of the private training in six weeks to come up with a longer-term viable cover. For the present, she'd given her mother a modified version of the truth: representatives of the federal government had debriefed her in Germany, offering a mountain retreat in order to recover from the terrorist attack.

Retreat. Yeah, right.

Olivia looked down at the evergreen-brocaded mountains below her. If her mother thought that running, swimming, and hiking counted as therapeutic, then it hadn't been a lie.

The private camp turned out to be as rustic as Olivia had imagined. What she hadn't imagined was the competition vying for Starling's team. A tall, sturdy blonde named Lily Crane immediately stood out. She looked like a middle on a college volleyball team, the tallest woman who dominated the blocks *and* the hits.

Given her last name, Olivia deduced that Lily already worked for Starling. Given her overt hostility, and Olivia was certain that the other woman wanted the new mission *and* had identified her main rival. She reacted as soon as Olivia showed up at Eagle's Nest, as Sam referred to the camp, clearly trying to put Olivia on defense from the outset. They shared a dorm-style cabin with two other women, and Lily made sure that Olivia got a top bunk—and a heaping of nasty practical jokes, like the used tampon on her pillow and the salt in her morning juice.

Olivia had handled this before. In middle school.

She ignored Lily as best she could and focused on the lessons that Sam oversaw.

The dozen women training at Eagle's Nest began their mornings with a sprint through the woods over a rough-cleared trail. The uneven terrain had been modified to remove hidden obstacles, rocks, and downed trees as well as ankle-twisting rabbit holes, but Sam assured them that it was still dangerously challenging even if the goal was primarily physical conditioning.

"It also calls on your powers of observation," he said after the first daily run. "It's not something to run on auto-pilot. And no one gets extra points for being first."

It was the only warning he gave that the trail held surprises for the unwary.

After finishing the trail, they grabbed chow in the main building, which looked like a barn from the outside but on the inside held a small dining area, kitchen in back, and a training arena in the main room that also doubled as a classroom with a large conference table in the corner.

Then they'd spend the morning learning about terrorist-financing networks, money laundering, and geography of critical regions. In the afternoon, they practiced shooting, either at targets on a range set up in a cleared meadow, or at each other in the woods on opposing teams. When they were already mentally and physically tired, a hard, muscled man called Tank trained them in the arena in Krav Maga, the Israeli mixed-martial art. Olivia, still healing, worked one-on-one with Sam, who taught her techniques for defending her injured side during hand-to-hand combat.

From this schedule, Olivia learned a few critical things. One, the other women already had years of military and intelligence experience. Two, someone—she was sure it was Lily—actively sabotaged her training. One morning, as she led the sprint, she almost stepped into a hole in the middle of the trail that had been cleverly hidden under a layer of soil.

And three, Sam Ahren was a gentleman who wouldn't take advantage of Olivia's weak side to win a bout, no matter how much she pushed him.

But Lily Crane had no such compunction.

"You don't do her any favors, Uncle," she said as she watched from the side while Olivia and Sam circled each other. "*Jihadis* have no problem stoning their women. They won't care that she's wounded."

Olivia and Sam ignored Lily, who persisted. "Hey, princess, hurt yourself while surfing on summer break?"

Olivia pulled up short and faced the other woman, her hands still guarding her face. "C'mon, then. Show me what you'd do to take this princess down."

"Olivia," said Sam, stepping between them. "That's not a good idea."

Olivia swiveled her gaze to hold Sam's. "I think it is," she said. "She's not going to stop until she finds out what I'm made of. I can handle her. Or I don't deserve to be here."

Whatever Sam saw in Olivia's gaze convinced him. He nodded and stepped back.

Olivia, who'd watched the other woman for the past three weeks, anticipated Lily's aggressive assault as he did. She danced back, energy coursing through her at this new challenge. The hard light in Lily's gaze said that the other woman had every intention of hurting her. Badly. A broken leg, a broken arm, a concussion. Whatever it took to eliminate Olivia from training.

The other blonde, heavier by thirty pounds and half a head taller, rushed past Olivia, just missing her with a raised forearm aimed at her throat.

Olivia rammed her elbow into Lily's upper back. As Lily stumbled, Olivia stomped on the back of her knee. Lily crumpled to the ground, but as she went down, she wrapped an arm around Olivia's thigh. They tumbled together to the mat with Olivia underneath.

In an instant, Olivia was back on the Ibiza beach under the terrorist choking her. Panic surged through her. Bucking, she managed to lift Lily, rolling over onto the other woman's torso before capturing one of her arms with a thigh. Lily swung her free elbow at Olivia's head, landing a blow to her cheekbone.

The pain cleared the panic fogging Olivia's mind. Time slowed down.

Leaning forward in the mount, she wrapped her legs around Lily's upper thighs and hooked her ankles together. At the same time, she forced an arm under Lily's neck and wrapped it around her, pulling her tight into a choke hold.

Lily bucked and tried to push Olivia's legs from hers, but Olivia clung to her.

Then Lily punched Olivia's healing side. Agony tore through Olivia. Blackness washed through her vision. Her ankles unlocked, and she slipped forward, freeing Lily's legs. Lily bucked again and began to roll ...

Until Olivia slid her knees into Lily's armpits, leaning her shoulder into the other woman's head. As Lily's face twisted to the side, Olivia inserted her fist between them, pressing it into Lily's throat with the weight of her chest.

Lily pounded on the mat, signaling her submission, but Olivia held the position several seconds longer. Gasping and sputtering, Lily sat up. Olivia herself would have collapsed onto the mat except that Sam extended a large, warm hand to pull her to her feet.

"Where'd you learn to do that?" he asked, surprise in his voice.

Olivia shrugged as one of the other trainees handed her a bottle of water. "Watching you and Tank grapple." At his intake of breath, she added, "I'm a fast study." Her voice broke at the sharp twinge that knifed through her.

"Let's get you to the medic," said Sam before turning to Lily, who'd just shrugged off Tank's helping hand. "By the way, this 'princess' who just kicked your ass? A *jihadi* stabbed her in Ibiza. I think she's earned a few favors. As for you, pack your bag. You're off my team."

FIVE

At the end of August, Sam formed two smaller teams from six of the remaining trainees, an alpha team and a bravo team. Olivia, assigned to Alpha Team with Monica and Julia, would approach Chase Graham with the intent to develop a relationship. She still hadn't formulated a good cover story to give her parents, although they already knew that she'd taken a leave of absence from Brown for the fall semester.

The day before the women packed up, Sam reviewed specific details related to Graham, who lived in Washington, D.C. Olivia said nothing while several of the other women catcalled and whistled at the images of the young financier that Sam had projected on a screen next to the conference table.

Instead, she studied Chase's face for any hint about his character and personality beyond that of celebrity bachelor. She needed to tailor her approach to him, but nothing in the handsome features or expensive suit suggested anything to her.

"That's enough ogling the man cake. I feel violated already," said Sam, grinning. "Time to work out some details about the next stage. Olivia, Monica, and Julia, you three have an apartment in Bethesda. The rest of you will be next door in Chevy Chase on procurement, logistics, and cleanup—anything to make this mission run for the foreseeable future."

"What does Chase like to do for fun?" asked Olivia, flipping to the back of her mission brief to look at candid photos of the target. The others had quieted, their earlier banter evaporating as they focused on the screen.

"Golf," answered Monica, skimming through the papers in the folder in front of her. "Yachting and horseback riding. Something called 'curling.'"

"From the looks of his physique in these gym photos, I'd say he curls about 110 pounds," said Tara, Bravo Team's logistics and procurement expert, from the other side of the table.

"When he's not engaged in sporting activities, he's an asset manager for Graham Asset Management, a subsidiary of Graham Investments licensed by the SEC. Right now, Chase's primary client is a private equity fund run by his father, Charles, that buys biotech startups. Last year Chase made two million dollars on that fund alone." This info on their target came from Julia, whose background in finance had almost assured her a place on alpha team.

Olivia was grateful for her new teammate's expertise because she suspected that Chase's financial shenanigans was the area that would give her the most trouble on this mission. That, and Chase's lifestyle. Her own was decidedly middleclass, despite some of the pursuits that her parents had managed to pay for during her adolescence.

Both teams continued to review Chase's profile, which contained some very specific details, including the number of women he brought back to his Victorian Row Home in DuPont Circle and his favorite single-malt whisky, Lagavulin. He'd played point guard on Georgetown's basketball team and spent an inordinate amount of time with his former teammates, clubbing and hanging in sports bars. However—and this was definitely a surprise—he spent many Saturday mornings at a food kitchen and most Saturday nights at the symphony or opera.

He also donated to a veritable portfolio of charities.

She focused on an image of Chase in a tuxedo at a charity event. "Graham has season tickets to the New York Met as well as the National Symphony Orchestra." She paused and looked up at Sam, before addressing the rest of the team. "There's our in. My NOC should have something to do with music performance."

"I take it that's something you can pull off?" asked Monica, who now leaned back in her chair, arms crossed, miming indifference or the callowness of the jock.

Olivia knew better. Monica liked to listen very intently to what was going on around her. She'd absorb all of the information being discussed, internalize it, and then have an insight that no one else had.

Olivia wondered if Monica would argue that she should take lead on the mission given that she was Alpha Team's resident athlete—she'd herself been a small forward for Tennessee, a college basketball powerhouse that went to the NCAA tournament every year, including winning Monica's freshman year.

Besides that, Monica was the same age as Chase and very attractive in a fresh, natural way with luxurious honey-brown hair and brown eyes.

It wouldn't be a bad call. Not at all.

Olivia sat up and looked at Monica as she answered the question about a music NOC. "Yes." She studied Monica's expression, but all she read was disinterest. "I sang soprano all through high school, going to All Nationals in choir. I could have gone to conservatory, but I chose pre-med instead. If we find the right profile, I can sell it. But what about you? You two have basketball in common, and Graham spends a lot of time with his old basketball buddies. You could approach him."

"I don't think Graham is interested in dating another basketball player," said Monica, nodding at the projected image. "Something tells me he's maintaining a certain profile by keeping in touch with his old college buddies. Like Bruce Wayne. But his Saturday activities are all his own. Notice he never goes out on the weekends with his friends?"

Now Fiona, Bravo Team's sniper and demolitions expert, spoke. "And the women he takes to those Saturday events are all model-perfect blondes. You're his type, Liv."

Sam, who'd stood quietly to the side while they discussed the situation, stepped closer to the table. "It's good to explore options, but Monica's right, Olivia. You're the one to cultivate a relationship with Graham."

He looked at the other women, who listened intently. "No offense, ladies, but you all reek a bit too much of the military. Graham will smell the rest of you a klick away. Olivia here looks like the ambitious college student she is. He's more likely to let his guard down with her."

Tess, Bravo Team's hacker and security expert, chose that moment to weigh in. "And I've got the perfect NOC for Olivia." She lifted her chin toward the screen, which she'd commandeered to show a Web page with an image of a red-brick mansion and the word *Strathmore* at the top.

"Strathmore is a center for the arts located in North Bethesda operated by Montgomery County. Its Music Center opened in 2005 in partnership with the Baltimore Symphony Orchestra. That same year, the Artist in Residence program, which targets musicians ages 16 to 32, launched to help them transition to professional careers. Each year, six are chosen during a very competitive process for a 10-month mentoring and performance program."

Tess paused to look at the rest of the team. "Lots of big-name philanthropists sponsor Strathmore, but Graham is an unnamed benefactor of the AIR program. He's also on the board of the Institute for Artistic Development which runs AIR. He spends a lot of time visiting the young musicians, away from the media circus that usually follows him at bigger profile events."

Olivia sat up, her spine tingling. The medal on her chest vibrated. When she touched it, it was very warm. "Now I know what will work for both my parents *and* Graham." She grinned in triumph. "I've decided to chuck my ambitions for medical school to return to my music studies."

Sam smiled. It was bright and wide in his tanned face. "Sounds like a perfect cover."

As Olivia had predicted, her parents accepted her change of college plans with equanimity. She'd left Eagle's Nest stronger and fitter than she'd ever been, and she'd stopped having nightmares that woke the whole house. Although they attributed it to the mountain retreat, her parents exuded relief. Her mother even admitted that she'd feared that Olivia had gotten so wound tight over her cousin's death and the subsequent terrorist attack that she might bury herself in her premed studies.

"You're so young, Olivia! Too young to stop living and forego some fun. I think this will be good for you, give you a little perspective. And if you want to return to medicine, you'll know it's what you really want."

Olivia hugged her mom, a pang going through her at the deceit. She wished she could tell her parents what she was doing, and that it was what she really wanted.

Instead, she told them that she'd made a couple of friends at the retreat, Julia and Monica, and that they were already planning to move in together in Bethesda.

And she used the long Labor Day weekend and the following week at home to practice piano and do voice exercises. Her mom wasn't wrong in one sense: it *was* good for her to sing and play again. She *had* cut that part of herself off after Emily's death.

Her dad helped her move into the Bethesda apartment where Julia and Monica were already in residence. He surprised her by hugging her tightly on the way out the door.

"You got this, sweet girl," he said into her ear. Olivia heard a catch in his voice. "Julia and Monica seem like levelheaded roommates. And you have the voice of an angel. It's a gift. You should use it."

A lump threatened to choke her. Olivia swallowed hard. "I will, Dad," she said before kissing him goodbye.

She'd have to use her musical gifts to catch Chase Graham's eye at Strathmore.

Julia, who'd been placed in a job in a financial services office as a personal advisor, had made sure that Olivia had a spot at Strathmore even though the enrollment period ended in mid-August. Monica had been placed as a field instructor in the Readiness Training Program at the Uniformed Services University, which educated medical personnel from all branches of the military.

Catching Chase Graham's eye at Strathmore turned out to be easier than anyone could have predicted. On Olivia's first Friday at the community arts center, Graham attended an open rehearsal in which Olivia sang a set of songs to introduce herself to the other music students.

Unlike the college student that Sam had described her as or the other twenty-somethings at Strathmore, she'd dressed in a vintage style, wearing a demure white blouse and long, straight dark skirt and four-inch black suede Christian Louboutin heels with black bows. She wore her hair in a loose chignon and a strand of antique pearls that Tara had found at an estate sale. Red lipstick the exact shade of the soles of her stilettos and black eyeliner completed the elegant, old-fashioned image she projected.

An image designed to attract attention.

Olivia didn't see Graham until she'd already begun singing 'La Vie en Rose,' an extremely popular French song from the post-World War II era. She'd sung it at her senior recital in high school, and Emily had adored it so much that she'd intended to sing it someday at her cousin's wedding. Instead, she sang it at Emily's funeral, tears streaming down her face.

Today Olivia sang in the original French, for the first time delivering an emotional performance in line with the song, which expressed hope after a dark period. A Strathmore violinist accompanied her, lending her performance a charming antique air.

Just as she sang *Et, dès que je l'aperçois*, that is, *And, when I see him,* Graham moved apart from the knot of teachers and students that had gathered around him in the back of the room, his gaze connecting with hers. Electricity jumped inside Olivia's chest, adding a genuine breathless note to the next two lines, *Alors je sens en moi, Mon coeur qui bat. Then I feel within me, my heart pounding.*

Graham's surveillance photos did nothing to convey the reality of the man.

He was tall, handsome, and dressed in tasteful but expensive casual clothing. He would have drawn everyone's gaze regardless. But he had a magnetic aura. And he seemed equally struck by her.

Olivia didn't know whether the nerves dancing along her skin stemmed from the mission or the instant chemistry between them.

The next thing Olivia knew, Graham strode along the outside of the chairs in the small recital hall, coming to a standstill at her feet, his smooth tenor joining her gentle soprano for the final romantic verses. For that brief span of time, their voices mingled in a surprisingly pleasing harmony.

Silence hushed the previously buzzing room, almost as if no one wanted to be responsible for breaking the spell of the impromptu duet.

"*Enchanté de vous rencontrer,*" said Graham, raising his hand. *Enchanted to meet you.*

He sounded like someone from another time. Like Prince Charming.

Olivia accepted, swallowing at the thrill that raced through her at Graham's touch, and let him guide her to the short steps down to the recital hall floor. For the first time since she'd accepted Starling's offer, she felt young and naïve. And out of her depth.

At 26, Graham had six years more than she did and a world of experience with women, beautiful, sophisticated women who still seemed to fall thrall to his attentions. Just last year, one of his former dates had been convicted of stalking him after she managed to circumvent his security and follow him into a restroom at a club.

When Olivia reached the floor, she found herself face-to-face with Graham, whose compelling green eyes warmed with a genuine smile that made them crinkle at the corner. He clearly smiled and laughed often.

"Hello," he said. His speaking voice pleased her ear as much as his singing voice. "I'm Chase. Who're you? And how long have you been at Strathmore? I don't recall seeing you before, and I'm here all the time."

The buzz in the room returned, more pronounced this time. No one had left yet, although this had been an informal event in the middle of the afternoon between lessons and group rehearsals.

"I'm Olivia. I just moved to Bethesda and discovered Strathmore in the local music scene and thought I'd give it a try," she said, aware that she was talking too quickly.

A small voice in the back of Olivia's brain told her the obvious: she was attracted to Chase Graham as she'd never been attracted to anyone before. It was doing funny things to her normally clear thinking.

"Good," said Chase, grinning. If his smile had fixed her focus, his infectious grin made her heart turn over.

Charlotte Dunning, the Institute's director, appeared at Chase's elbow. "Mr. Graham, I had no idea that you had such a beautiful singing voice! And your French accent and diction are impeccable. I don't suppose you'd like to sing at a Strathmore community concert?"

"Only if Olivia will reprise the duet with me," he said without taking his gaze from Olivia's. "I haven't wanted to sing in a long time, but she sings like an angel." But then he turned toward Charlotte and addressed her, "And *La Vie en Rose* is one of my favorite songs. Love makes even the darkest view rosy."

Charlotte made a surprised sound, which she covered with a chuckle. She looked at Olivia. "Well? Are you interested in singing with one of Strathmore's top donors?"

Even if Olivia hadn't been on a mission to get closer to Chase, she would have understood that she didn't have a choice here. Keeping donors happy was always an unstated priority at nonprofits.

She smiled, looking first at Charlotte and then back to Chase, who seemed to wait on her answer as if uncertain she'd accept.

"Of course," she said to both of them before smiling over at Chase again. "However, I must warn you, it's been a long time since I performed in front of a large audience. I don't want to make you look bad."

Chase laughed, throwing his head back and sounding delighted. "There's no way you could ever do that. The audience will be as beguiled by you as I am."

Olivia blushed and ducked her gaze toward the door, where a soldier in fatigues greeted one of the other students. She was instantly brought back to her mission.

"Then we'll need to rehearse," she said. "Maybe we can rehearse here?"

She glanced at Charlotte, who watched the interaction like a hawk with a slightly puzzled air. The director started to answer when Chase cut her off.

"It was good talking to you today, Charlotte." He nodded at the director, his tone and manner businesslike. "Call my office, and my assistant will set something up."

Chase was clearly dismissing the director, whose frown disappeared too quickly for Olivia to be sure that she'd seen it. Assuming that she'd also been dismissed, Olivia turned to leave, but Chase placed his hand on her upper arm to stop her. She felt the warmth of his palm all the way to her soles. A tiny shiver escaped her.

"Wait a moment, Olivia. I want to get your contact details. I have a piano at my place in D.C. We can rehearse there so no one can hear my mistakes. And so I can find out more about you." He grinned that heart-melting grin again.

Olivia told him her cellphone number, and Chase handed her his business card.

"Chase Graham?" she read aloud. "Why does that name sound so familiar?"

Now Chase turned serious. "I guess it was too much to hope that you've never heard of me. I, uh, unfortunately have something of a reputation."

He looked embarrassed, his gaze flitting away for a moment.

"Reputation?" she asked as she looked over his shoulder into the empty recital hall.

When had everyone else left?

For the first time in their interaction, Chase looked uncomfortable and a bit awkward.

He ran a hand through his light-brown hair, making its smooth strands stand upright in an endearing manner. "Um, maybe you recognize my name from the tabloids. Or MySpace."

"Or *People Magazine*'s Most Eligible Bachelor of 2007," said Olivia, smiling. She didn't think it was wise to play ignorant too long given Chase's iconic status in American society. "I don't really pay attention to the latest celebrity gossip"—which was true—"so I didn't recognize you right away." Which wasn't.

Chase blushed but held Olivia's gaze. "Guilty as charged. Does that make me more or less interesting as a duet partner?"

Olivia tilted her head, studying him while she thought this over. This side of her target totally took her off guard. He seemed to care what she thought about him. Chase Graham was a lot more complex than his CIA file portrayed. And not nearly as insufferable or hard to read as she'd feared.

Another shortcoming of relying on Open-Source Intelligence, or OSINT. Gathering intelligence via direct interpersonal inter-action, or HUMINT, filled in so much of the picture. She tucked that insight away before answering Chase's question.

"It makes you more interesting, definitely," she said and meant it.

"Then I'm glad." He smiled again.

No matter how many times she saw Chase's smile, Olivia doubted that she'd find it less appealing. If anything, it had be-come more engaging the more she spent time around him—and she'd only been in his presence for ten minutes!

Uneasiness washed through her. She'd likely be spending hours, if not days with Chase. What happened when their chemistry became too compelling to sidestep? Just exactly how did she play this? What would Sam tell her to do? She could guess what Starling would say. Thank God he wasn't running this operation.

The thought had hardly crossed Olivia's mind before Chase spoke again. "Because I want you to go to dinner with me. There's a wonderful little bistro I'd love to share with you. Say you'll join me. Please?"

Olivia swallowed, her smile wavering a bit. Rivulets of excitement pushed out the uneasiness, sending butterflies dancing in her stomach. She touched her medal with her fingertip to calm herself.

Then she answered in a steady voice. "Yes, of course. I'd love to."

Six

Olivia had assumed that Chase would drive them into D.C. to a fancy French restaurant somewhere in Dupont Circle.

She was wrong.

Instead, he drove her to her apartment for her passport and a weekend bag. While she was inside, he called a local airfield where his private jet waited on standby for impromptu jaunts. Monica and Julia hadn't returned from their cover jobs, so Olivia jotted a hasty note telling them where—and with whom—she would be that weekend. No one had expected her to make contact so quickly, and it had only been a curious impulse that had led her to dress the way she had for her brief recital.

Then she called Sam and left him a coded voicemail.

And, feeling like she was flying in more ways than one, Olivia let Chase fly her to Paris. Himself. He was also a pilot, which, he explained, made it a whole lot easier to leave on a moment's notice.

They got in late, but Chase had called ahead and booked two suites at the Bulgari Hotel. When he learned that Olivia had never been to

Paris, he determined on a whirlwind tour of the biggest sights. So the next morning they had coffee and croissants before embarking on a walking tour of the Champs-Élysées that included visiting the Arc d'Triomphe and the Eiffel Tower. Then, after a slow lunch at a sidewalk café, they took an hour-long cruise on the Seine.

What really surprised Olivia was the small Parisian bistro Chase took her to that evening. *Au Pied de Fouet*, or *At the Foot of the Whip*, didn't take reservations and had a line outside waiting to be seated when they arrived. While they waited, Chase peppered her with questions. Olivia's cover allowed her to answer naturally, and all was going well until Chase asked her why she'd moved to Bethesda and returned to her voice studies, which caught her off guard.

"How do you know that I've returned?" she asked, startled. And a little fearful.

"You said it had been sometime since you've performed in front of a large audience," he said. "And there's no way anyone would you let you keep that magnificent voice to yourself if you were taking voice lessons."

The *maître d'hôtel* appeared to escort them into the bistro before she could think of an answer, even though she'd practiced explaining her reasons for moving to Bethesda and beginning voice lessons again.

Olivia realized that she'd committed a cardinal intelligence sin: she'd let herself get caught up in the 'date' with Chase.

By the time they were seated, she'd gotten control of her wandering attention and answered smoothly and naturally.

The food in the bistro was delicious *and* inexpensive, a fact that surprised Olivia. The staff knew Chase and lavished attention on them, even going so far as to apologize that, because monsieur had never brought a companion before, they didn't have a special napkin for her!

After they'd shared a *tarte tatin*, an apple tart with a divine buttery crust, Chase paid the bill with far more cash than it required (though Olivia only knew this because she'd happened to read about the general exchange rate during Alpha Team's deep-dive of the private-equity-investment world). Then they strolled in the warm, late September evening, talking more about their favorite songs and music styles before moving on to books.

At last, when it was quite clear that she would arrive back in Bethesda in the wee hours of the morning, they returned to Chase's jet and flew home.

Olivia got approximately five hours of sleep before Sam showed up for an Alpha Team debrief Sunday morning. She stumbled into the kitchen where Monica had brewed a pot of coffee, and Julia had started frying bacon and eggs.

"You two are the best roomies," said Olivia, yawning as she poured a cup of coffee. She hadn't really been a coffee drinker until now, but she was starting to see the benefits.

"Well, we know how much hard work you put in, flying to Paris and back in less than two days," said Julia, fixing Olivia a plate that included strawberries and one of the muffins that Sam had brought.

"Yeah, it must have been killer on your feet to wear those Louboutin stilettos the whole time," said Monica, who preferred walking shoes and sturdy boots. "Unless Mr. Swept-You-Off-Your-Feet offered to carry you everywhere?"

"I'd say Olivia's the one who made a conquest," said Sam, sipping his coffee at the small breakfast table. "We've had eyes on Graham for months. He's got a recognizable routine and cadre of friends and dates. He's never done anything this spontaneous."

He waited until the three women sat down before starting the debrief. "We don't need to get into the details of the date, Olivia. Tara shadowed you all day while everyone else got into Graham's residence here and installed bugs and tapped his phone."

A spurt of surprise filled Olivia until she realized that, of course, one of the team would have been dispatched to Paris. And her cellphone provided enough tracking information to find them.

"Graham used the time in Paris to meet up with this guy."

Sam slid a photo from a manila folder across the table toward Olivia. It showed Chase and another man in a souvenir shop while Olivia browsed silk scarves in the background. A guilty pang pierced her. She hadn't noticed him interacting with anyone. And he'd bought her the scarf she'd chosen. It was still in her unpacked bag.

She lifted the photo so that Monica and Julia could see the dark-haired man. He looked vaguely Middle Eastern, but that didn't mean anything.

"Who is he?" asked Olivia, not waiting on the rebuke of her situational awareness. Or rather lack thereof. "I don't recognize him. And I would have known if Cha–Graham had spoken to anyone."

"Call him Chase," said Sam, watching her. "You're allowed. In fact, I insist. You're developing a relationship with him. Just be careful not to let his extravagant lifestyle distract you from the mission."

Translation: it's not personal. Don't fall for the target.

Olivia wanted to squirm. She'd never been chastised for slacking on an assignment. Instead, she lifted her chin, squared her shoulders, and said, "Copy that."

Sam gave a sharp nod and went on. "The answer to your first question is that's Saad Abadi, a known Saudi arms broker. As for the second implied question, it was a modified brush pass. Although both men were at the same location at the same time, the real exchange took place when Graham purchased the guidebook that Abadi planted intel inside."

At this point, Sam passed over several photos taken of the two men. Abadi picking up a guidebook in one, and several frames later, Chase purchasing the same guidebook.

"Tara has great instincts by the way. She shot those photos before Tess identified Abadi." He sipped his coffee and then returned to the subject of Oliva's budding relationship with Chase. "They say a picture's worth a thousand words. From what I've seen, I'd say you've gotten closer to Graham faster than we could've hoped."

As he said this, Sam pulled out front-page tabloid articles showing a picture of her talking with Chase after the recital. Someone had used a now-ubiquitous cellphone camera to document them together. Olivia had to agree: they both looked a little smitten. And given Chase's stature, the tabloids had responded in a frenzy of speculation.

"Dunning cornered him into singing a duet with me," said Olivia. "Apparently he's not just a music lover but a singer as well."

"That means rehearsing together?" Julia grinned. "How convenient."

Olivia nodded. "He's going to call later this week to set up our first rehearsal."

"What happens when he looks into her and finds that she survived the Ibiza attack?" asked Monica now, honing in on a weak point in the media exposure.

Sam's expression turned opaque. "That's up to Olivia. Only she can get a read on Chase and respond as necessary."

"Do we know why Grah—Chase is doing this? Funding terrorists?" asked Olivia, taking a sip of coffee to hide what she knew were conflicted feelings in her gaze. "It's hard to square with the man I met."

"Are you asking how an All-American basketball player from a Catholic family and a Jesuit university justifies aiding religious fundamentalists bent on killing American citizens? Who knows? Who cares?" Now Sam sounded angry. He leaned forward. "You read Graham's file."

Olivia had. They all had.

Sam continued. "He gives investment advice and manages private equity accounts for the unindicted co-conspirators of the Holy Land Five."

After more than 15 years of international investigation led by the FBI, the U.S. Government had leveled 108 counts against the purported U.S.-based charity claiming that it had funneled almost $13 million to Hamas.

"Speaking of," said Julia, slicing through the tension and bringing them back on topic. "We couldn't access Graham's work email, but we were able to get into his assistant Clark's personal account. From there, we accessed Graham's schedule. He's got a meeting set next week with the director of development for the Islamic Society for North America, Ghassan Mousa. There's been chatter in other channels that suggests ISNA has plans for its upcoming fundraiser, namely a shipment of SAMs."

Sam sat upright. "We need to get more information about that meeting. How does Olivia get it for us?"

"If she can access Graham's personal computer, I can get her a thumb drive with a utility program that can get inside his firewall and give us remote access," said Julia. "I can also take control of his phone if he uses it to check email."

"Good." Sam finished his coffee and stood. "You and Tess keep digging into the biotech equity fund. Find a thread and pull it. It's as true today as it was in Al Capone's day: forensic accounting will be the key to bringing down the backbone of the terrorist network."

"Let me know as soon as you get a rehearsal date with Graham. Bugs and surveillance can't beat eyes and ears inside his place in Dupont Circle."

He didn't say anything else, but the implication was clear: forensic accounting might be fine for putting someone in prison. It wouldn't prevent another terrorist attack.

The next day, Julia caught Olivia as she was heading out to Strathmore.

"Here," she said, handing Olivia a thumb drive with the incursion software utility. "The program automatically downloads once the drive is plugged in. It will take ninety seconds to install, but you can remove the drive after thirty seconds."

Olivia nodded and tucked it into her big leather shoulder bag. She was about to pass by Julia for the door, when her teammate laid a hand on her arm.

"Hey, Olivia. You got this. Just get me into his PC. I'll take it from there. Once I'm in, I can flag suspicious accounts, and then the Feds will freeze them so no money can be withdrawn. What with ISNA's 'unindicted co-conspirator' designation, Graham won't suspect that you had anything to do with it."

Something eased in Olivia's chest at Julia's pep talk.

"Thanks," she said, pressing Julia's hand with her own.

However, Olivia didn't hear from Graham until Friday morning.

"Hey," he said after she answered his call, "sorry to get back to you so late in the week. It's been crazier around here than usual. I just got off the phone with Charlotte. She talked me into hosting a benefit concert for Strathmore with us as the headliners. 'Killing two birds with one stone,' is how she phrased it. Do you mind?" He sounded like he genuinely cared what she thought.

"Of course not," said Olivia, wondering if any of his ISNA clients would be at the concert.

"Great! My assistant tells me that it's better to do this before the holiday season, so that leaves us roughly six weeks to put together a program and audition Strathmore students. And, of course, we'll need to rehearse a few times. Can you make it tomorrow by chance?"

Olivia's heart skipped a beat. She bit her lip to steady herself before answering, "Hm. I was planning to spend the day with the roommates ..."

"I'll make it worth your while," said Chase as she trailed off. "Come at two, and I'll feed you dinner afterwards."

Excellent! Olivia didn't let herself question whether it was because she'd have more time to access Chase's computer or because it felt like a date.

"Well, then, when you put it like that, how can a poor student resist?" she asked, letting a teasing note hide her excitement.

The next day she drove to Dupont Circle in the 1988 Honda Civic sedan that Tara had scoured the greater D.C. area to find. Something that screamed responsible-but-not-a-lot-of-money that a music student from the Boston suburbs drove. Chase had directed her to park in a nearby garage where he had a long-term lease for parking spaces.

She felt self-conscious parking what had seemed like a respectable car until she pulled into the reserved spot.

Chase's Victorian, however, made her feel more comfortable.

The young financier answered the door himself. In his casual long-sleeved pullover and chinos, he looked less like a high-powered investment manager and more like the young man he was.

Olivia handed Chase the flowers and wine she'd brought and followed him inside.

"Who decorated?" she asked, looking around as he led her off the entryway where a baby grand piano had pride of place in the round tower overlooking the corner of Swann Street NW.

"Why?" he asked, glancing over his shoulder at her. "Doesn't look like a bachelor lives here? My mom sent over her decorator and told him that he needed to make it friendly for females because she wants grandchildren."

A pang pierced Olivia. What was Chase's mother going to think when she learned that she'd never have grandchildren from him?

"You can put your purse and jacket there," he said, gesturing to a comfortable chair in the nearby living room. "Juliana, my housekeeper, will have a fit, but she's not here today. It's just you and me." He grinned at her, before carrying the flowers and wine to the kitchen.

They rehearsed *La Vie en Rose* and then took turns playing and singing their favorites from memory for the rest of the afternoon, generating ideas for a concert program. And all the time, Olivia was running through scenarios for finding and hacking Chase's laptop without getting caught. It wasn't until he declared that it was time to start dinner—which he intended to cook for her—that Olivia had a chance to leave Chase's company. As soon as she could, she excused herself to go to the powder room, which was out of sight of the kitchen.

She prowled around the dining room, but no laptop was tucked inside the sideboard.

Then she returned to the living room which opened into the tower room, scanning niches and dark corners that her earlier review had missed. She'd seen his laptop on the flight to Paris, but the worn leather messenger bag must be elsewhere.

She was going to have to drug Chase to give her enough time to visit the other three floors of the Victorian townhouse.

Almost as soon as Olivia realized this, framed pictures among art objects and collectibles on built-in shelves along one side of the room caught her interest. She approached for a closer look, her gaze honing in on an image of Chase wearing a tuxedo among a group of people.

One of them was Ghassan Mousa.

She picked up the photo to study it. Mousa laughed, a large, open-mouthed laugh that lit his dark eyes. His hand rested on Chase's shoulder. Chase looked young—and less haunted. She couldn't say why she thought that.

Olivia gripped the picture, both at this evidence of consorting with a terrorist so boldly displayed in Chase's living room and the spurt of anguish she felt on his behalf. Something urged her to look at the photo's back, to discover whether anything had been inscribed. She flipped the frame over and slid the cardboard easel off.

Only to find a listening device. Not one of theirs.

Shocked, she stared at it for a moment.

Then she heard Chase's footsteps from the kitchen. Hurriedly she slid the easel into the frame before he appeared in the room.

"There you are. I was beginning to think you'd been snatched," said Chase with a grin. Then he saw what she was holding. His grin faltered but returned—just not to his eyes. "What are you doing? Spying on me?"

Olivia's heart thumped. Out of nowhere, *Sensei* Mark's voice assured her that she needed to ask questions to find out if her cover really was blown.

Swallowing as Chase approached, his hand out for the picture, Olivia said, "I'm sorry. I didn't mean to pry. I just wanted to know more about you. Then I saw you wearing this tux and wondered if it was a Strathmore event. I recognize the ceiling lights from the concert hall."

Chase, a slight frown pulling his eyes together, gazed at the photo as if for the first time.

"I'd forgotten that," he said almost to himself. He set the picture back on the shelf. "Yes, that was my very first Strathmore fundraiser. We raised enough to cover all of the seats in the hall."

He looked at her. "Sorry. I'm just a little touchy. The most-eligible-bachelor thing gets a lot of interest from journalists. The *wealthy*-bachelor thing attracts even more eager women."

Olivia let her breath out slowly. She decided to press her luck and ask about Mousa. "You and the guy with his arm around your shoulder seem to have really hit it off."

Chase stiffened. A muscle jumped in his jaw. The sunny disposition she'd come to associate with him evaporated.

"Hardly," he said. He changed the subject. "Listen, I came to tell you that the local paparazzi got alerted that you're here with me. If you stay any longer, they'll swarm you when you leave. Raincheck on dinner? I can show you how to avoid the bulk of the photographers by going out the back door."

And like that, Olivia's opportunity to install the incursion software on Chase's laptop had vanished. It seemed unlikely she'd get another chance before the meeting with Mousa on Tuesday.

She'd failed her mission objective.

Nodding, she let Chase help her into her jacket before following him to the deck and downstairs to the carport where a blue door led outside to the street.

"Give me five minutes to get to the front door to distract them, then go," he said. He didn't even look at her.

"Hey," she said, laying her hand on his forearm as he grasped the doorknob. "I enjoyed rehearsing with you. I'm sorry I can't stay for dinner."

At that, Chase looked at Olivia. The haunted look in his eyes had intensified, leeching the green into celadon. "Me, too. Olivia."

It sounded like he meant that he regretted ever meeting her.

SEVEN

After Olivia failed to get access to Chase's laptop, Sam called an all-hands meeting at a secure location outside Bethesda. Starling had sent along up-to-the-minute intel about an Egyptian arms dealer, Lukman Kader, who'd met with Abadi two days before in Marseille.

Kader supplied SAMs to Hezbollah. ISNA's plans had taken a step closer to reality.

The team had less than 72 hours to come up with a plan to surveil the encounter between Graham and Mousa, which would take place at a D.C. restaurant owned by Palestinian immigrants known to donate to ISNA and other organizations with ties to Hamas.

And they needed to learn more about the other players watching Chase at the same time.

They'd been careful the first time they entered his house, going in during the night he and Olivia flew to Paris, though they couldn't be sure that Chase's surveillance had no knowledge of their visit. This time, however, they'd need a reason to get Chase out of the building for several hours while they swept it for other listening devices. Ideally, he—and his watchers—would have no reason to suspect anything.

"That's easy," said Tara, eating a green apple as she sat with her feet up on the coffee table of the house that they met in Saturday night. She looked tired after a week of overnight shifts outside Chase's Victorian. "Gas leak clears the neighborhood. And is easy to fake with a supply of mercaptan. Washington Gas along with D.C. police and fire will take care of the rest for us."

Bravo Team, which had already been on round-the-clock surveillance of Chase, would run the operation. They'd get in to the townhouse after the fire department ordered the power to the block shut off to prevent an explosion, deactivating his high-end security system for them. They'd leave the bugs so that the watchers would be unaware that they'd been discovered. If possible, they'd rule out domestic sources of surveillance.

But the signs pointed to foreign actors. No one speculated, yet Olivia knew what they were all thinking. *Mossad*. The FBI wasn't known for its covert finesse even in the States. The whole world knew it had been investigating the Holy Land Five and its conspirators for the better part of two decades. The Israelis wouldn't want to wait for American justice, even for one of its citizens. There was a very good chance that Chase had a target on his back already.

Sam turned to Julia and Tess. "You're sure there's no tap on his phones?"

Julia shook her head. "Not a soft tap through the phone company or mobile carrier at any rate. Neither local or federal law enforcement are eavesdropping on his calls. That doesn't rule out a hard tap on the landline at the residence or on the PBX at Graham Investments' office building."

"It wouldn't matter anyway. Graham's careful," said Tess. "I saw him using a high-end Blackberry last week instead of his regular cellphone. I'm sure that he keeps his communications with Mousa and the others separate from his personal and business lines, just like he stays off the internet at home."

"Nevertheless, someone else is watching him. Monica, Julia, go back to Graham Investments' offices and scour any place connected to Graham, especially his assistant's office. And check the PBX as well as the landline wiring at his house. This smells like another intelligence operation. If we hacked the assistant's email, you can bet the other operatives have bugged his office."

"Copy that," said Monica. "What about the laptop?"

"What do you think?" asked Sam in response.

"We'll get the incursion software installed, Uncle," said Julia. She threw a swift, sympathetic glance at Olivia. "Tess has the same utility. We'll have full access to Graham Investment's network by morning."

"Okay, everyone. You've got your orders. Comms open. Check in when you're on site."

Olivia's teammates nodded and began standing to gather their things, avoiding chitchat as they left. They'd practiced similar scenarios often at Eagle's Nest. They'd breach the DuPont Circle address and Graham Investments within the hour.

Olivia waited, aware that she'd been left out of the assignment—and not just because they couldn't risk her being spotted at either scene.

She was being sent to the principal's office.

After the front door to the ranch house shut behind Monica, who nodded once at Olivia before she left, Sam sighed and stood. He went into the kitchen and returned with two tumblers and a bottle of single-malt whisky.

The heavy glass tumblers clinked as he set them on the coffee table between them. He poured whisky in both and raised one to Olivia.

She blinked and said, "I'm not 21."

Sam tilted his head in a *Really?* manner.

Olivia accepted the tumbler and sipped the whisky. She was surprised at how doing that eased the tension she felt. She took another, larger sip. The liquid heat flowed to her stomach and then radiated outward.

"You like him," Sam said, watching her. At her mute nod, he asked, "Are you going to be able to complete the mission?"

That shocked Olivia. She hesitated. She suspected that any other handler would either demand an explanation or give her a warning. Sam had done neither. She owed it to him to be honest.

She held Sam's gaze. "If the mission is to disrupt funds flowing from the United States into the coffers of terrorists buying SAMs, yes."

"But you have doubts about Graham." It wasn't a question.

Still Olivia hesitated.

Sam's gaze never wavered. "Talk to me, Olivia. HUMINT is the best intelligence there is, bar none. And you're our best source of that. Right now, the case against Graham is very strong. Almost unbelievably strong. But it's all based on circumstantial evidence. A *lot* of it, to be frank. But that doesn't mean there isn't something we're not seeing."

Olivia looked into the whisky remaining in her tumbler. She wanted to swallow it, pour another full glass, and swallow that.

Instead, she lifted her face and squared her shoulders.

"It's more a feeling than anything," she said.

Sam waited.

"When he found me with the photo of him and Mousa, he seemed ... I don't know, surprised to see it on his shelf. When I asked if he and Mousa had hit it off, he said, 'Hardly.' In the next breath, he told me I had to leave. I guess the obvious explanation is that he's being cagey, maybe even suspects me. But it doesn't feel that way."

Sam didn't laugh or dismiss her conviction. Nor did he get angry as he had earlier. "How does it feel?"

"Like there's more to the story—a lot more—than bank records can tell."

"Okay, then," said Sam nodding. He drained his whisky and poured them each another draft. "Sounds like you have your next objective: cultivate an asset."

Olivia frowned. "Turn Chase? Surely that will take a lot longer than Tuesday."

Sam shrugged and sipped his whisky. "We never brought it up as a mission objective, but turning a key player, especially one enmeshed in such a complex network, should always be an option."

"Copy that," said Olivia.

"Besides, something tells me that you're going to be much better at asset development than hacking and eavesdropping."

Olivia's cellphone buzzed. She glanced at the screen.

"Speak of the devil. It's Chase. It's awfully late for him to call."

"Answer it."

Sam got up while Olivia took the call, but she knew he listened as she spoke.

Something in Chase's voice when she answered made the back of her neck tingle. She sat up, focusing on the call and dismissing Sam from her thoughts completely.

"Olivia, hi. Sorry if I caught you at a bad time. I know it's after midnight ... you're probably out ... I can call you back tomorrow. I was just going to leave you a voicemail."

"No, it's all right," she said, infusing warmth into her voice. "I was with friends, but I was just saying my goodbyes. What's up?"

Chase sighed audibly. "Nothing really ... I've just been thinking about what an asshole I was when I practically shoved you out the door earlier. I didn't even feed you dinner as I promised. It's been weighing on me."

He slurred the last sentence. Just a little bit. Apparently, he'd been drinking. Not enough that most people would notice, but Olivia had always had sensitive hearing.

"Would you like to come over to my place and talk?"

When he didn't answer immediately, Olivia added, "Don't worry. My roommates are both out for the rest of the night. It'll be just you and me. Do you like tea? It helps when talking to friends about serious subjects."

That must have been the right thing to say because Chase said, "Sure. How long will you be? I need to take care of a few things and grab my car, but I can be in Bethesda in forty-five minutes."

"That's perfect. I'll text you the address."

After Olivia ended the call, she looked up to see Sam leaning in the doorway to the kitchen, his arms crossed.

"Someone must be looking out for you. Graham practically walked into your arms."

Olivia drained her whisky and stood. Despite the second shot, she felt clearheaded and alert, as if the alcohol had evaporated through her pores before reaching her blood.

"He's not there yet, but I'll do my best to use this golden opportunity." She paused. "Thanks, Uncle."

She didn't need to explain. Sam just nodded.

"I want a sitrep as soon as he leaves. No matter what time it is."

Chase arrived at Olivia's apartment around two a.m. Bravo Team had waited until he'd returned to pick up his car before releasing the mercaptan. By a lucky turn of events, it was Chase who called in the gas leak to the local fire station. Tara had planned to call anonymously, but Chase's report as a resident carried a lot more weight. Rather than an initial investigation to confirm the leak, the police arrived and started banging on doors to evacuate the residents for a block around the source. It also meant that Chase would be in no hurry to return to his house.

Olivia had changed into baggy jersey pants and a long-sleeve T-shirt by the time he arrived, her hair in a loose braid over one shoulder. She'd slipped a batch of frozen cookie dough onto a baking sheet, filling the apartment with the sweet scent of chocolate and sugar. She'd gotten the idea from something her mother, a realtor, had once told her: scents work subtle magic, and the smell of baking cookies always made an open house more successful.

She had to admit, once she'd guided Chase to a seat at the small dining table next to the kitchen, he seemed to relax with every step.

"Just let me put the kettle on," she said, smiling at him as she gestured toward a chair. "I hope you don't mind the cookies. I picked up some bad habits during college."

"Not at all," said Chase, glancing around him in open curiosity.

Olivia knew from his file that he'd never lived in either a dorm or apartment complex.

After turning on the burner under the full kettle, she returned to the table where two Brown University mugs (nicely chipped and worn, thanks to Tara's diligence to detail), a simple porcelain plate from a set sourced from the local discount department store, and a box of grocery-store teabags waited.

Chase, a teabag dangling from one hand, sat reading the back of the box.

"Sorry, those are pretty generic. Poor student here. I can get you something else if you want."

Olivia turned to grab the sugar bowl on the counter behind her. When she turned back, Chase put a hand on her arm as she set it on the table.

"I don't care about the tea. In fact, I'm looking forward to trying it." After saying this, he dropped the bag into his mug with a flourish.

"Well, okay then." Olivia sat down across from him.

Chase, instead of pulling his hand back, took both of hers in his. The table was so small that his long arms spanned it without straining. Olivia felt the erratic pulse at his wrist, but his warm, dry palms engulfed hers.

They sat this way for several long moments. Chase appeared deep in thought. Olivia waited, aware that he wrestled with something momentous. She didn't expect what he said next, however.

"How did you do it? How did you fight the terrorists in Ibiza?" When Chase spoke, his voice sounded as rough as sandpaper. "What was it like to see all those people gunned down? To fear for your life—to get stabbed?"

The detachment she'd striven to maintain in his presence fled.

Olivia blinked and sat upright. Her own pulse pounded in her ears. "How do you know about that?" she asked. Her voice sounded strangled.

Holy crap, how had he thrown her off balance just by asking about Ibiza?

Because it means he really did look into you, a small voice inside her whispered. *Him, or his terrorist connections.*

An icy rivulet ran down her back.

Chase looked up and held her gaze. His green eyes glittered. "I looked into you, Olivia. Are you really so shocked? Being one of the Most Eligible Bachelors means I have a private investigator on speed dial. I wasn't always so careful." He sounded bitter when he said this.

That's your opening, said *Sensei* Mark's voice in Olivia's head.

Olivia swallowed and let a long breath out. "Because you didn't look into someone you should have?" she asked.

Chase shook his head.

The tea kettle whistled.

When she didn't move, afraid to break the spell, Chase asked, "Are you going to get that?" and dropped her hands.

"Yes, of course!" Olivia stood and went to take the kettle from the stove.

He followed her into the small kitchen. "Maybe I should go."

Olivia turned, the kettle in one hand. "I was terrified, Chase. But angry, too. If you looked into me, you know my cousin Emily was murdered. All I could think while I stood on that beach in Ibiza watching those bastards spraying tourists with bullets was that I *had* to do something."

"That's what I'm thinking too."

The oven timer sounded. Before Olivia could respond, Chase stepped closer and opened the door. Looking at her, he asked, "Where's your oven mitt?"

Mutely, Olivia opened a drawer and pulled out a mitt. Julia had purposefully singed the tip. She handed it to him. Chase pulled the tray out, and when he shot her a questioning look, she gestured toward the stove. By tacit agreement, they spent the next few minutes regaining their composure while filling mugs with hot water and the plate with cookies.

Finally, they sat down. Olivia asked nonchalantly as she dunked a teabag into hot water, "Would you like to see it? My scar?"

Chase, who'd dropped a couple of chocolate-chip cookies on a plate, brought his head up as if scenting prey. "Only if you're comfortable showing it to me."

Olivia dropped the teabag on her plate. Holding his gaze with hers, she lifted the edge of her T-shirt to expose her abdomen. A long, shiny-pink scar marred the smooth skin.

Chase stared at it before lifting a tentative fingertip to trace its length. When he'd finished, he sat up, ran a hand through his hair, and then squared his shoulders and held her gaze.

"That guy, the one in the photo you asked about today ... he–we are *not* friends. I met him at that charity event, the one for the new music center. He donated to the fund I set up for the AIR program when no one else had yet, even got a number of his friends to donate. Then he asked me to do some small favors that are technically against the rules, but I couldn't see the harm."

"Until he asked you to do something big and illegal," said Olivia, "reminding you that you'd already broken any number of laws already."

Chase nodded. "That's how I started laundering money for terrorists, who now threaten anyone close to me. They know about you, Olivia. I didn't think they paid any attention to the women I dated, but then Ghassan—he's the guy in the photo—called me today. He wants me to keep seeing you. He loves the idea that a woman who survived an attack by *jihadis* ends up dating their money man."

He picked up Olivia's hand where it rested on the table between them. The overhead light caused shadows to play over his features, emphasizing the fatigue. And something like despair.

"I really like you, Olivia. I mean, a *lot*. That's why, when Ghassan called and told me about you and the paparazzi, whom he sent to catch us together, I needed to get you out of the house. But I owe you an explanation for why we can't see each other anymore. It's just not safe. They're watching me. I can't drag you into the mess I've made of my life."

He dropped her hand.

Without conscious thought, Olivia touched a fingertip to the warm St. Michael medal on her chest.

"I don't think I would have survived Ibiza without a guardian angel," she said, realizing as she did that she meant it. "Something warned me before the terrorists got to the beach. And then American spec-ops soldiers arrived just in time to save my life. I think maybe that's why I'm here now, with you."

Chase frowned. "What do you mean?"

Olivia leaned forward, holding his gaze so that he couldn't mistake her. "Chase, I work for the CIA. I've been assigned to get close to you. They know you're laundering money for terrorists."

Chase reared back as if she'd struck him. "What?"

Olivia nodded. "It looks bad on paper for you, Chase. Mousa and the others have shielded themselves and left you exposed. The thing is, forensic accounting doesn't reveal motive or manipulation. Right now, you look like someone who wants to kill tourists on beaches."

"Oh, my God." Chase leaned his face into his hands.

"Hey." Olivia pulled one of his hands away. When he looked at her, she said, "I can help you. Instead of breaking up with me, bring me to lunch on Tuesday."

Shock washed over Chase's face. He blinked. "You know about the meeting?" he whispered.

Olivia nodded again. "We have intel that Hamas is currently negotiating to buy SAMs with funds from ISNA. We don't know the target yet though. We need eyes and ears inside the terrorist network. Get me closer to Mousa. Help me find a way to stop this sale. It's the only way to make something good come from all this."

"That sounds dangerous as hell."

"That's because it is." Olivia shrugged. "That's what I signed up for."

"No, I mean, dangerous for *me*. I never wanted to work with terrorists. They compelled me. What will happen if they find out I'm working with the CIA?"

Olivia narrowed her eyes and focused on Chase. She didn't like what she was going to say next, but it needed to be said. "Listen to me, and listen good. You can't just stick your head in the sand. You're already in danger, and not just from the terrorists. If the U.S. thinks you're guilty, what does the rest of the world think? I was recruited specifically to get access to the terrorist network through you. What do you think other countries might do to stop the flow of money? I can't promise you'll be safe, Chase. But right now, I'm the best chance you have."

Heavy silence filled the air. A faint clicking came from the twenty-year-old stove. Overhead, the incandescent light hummed.

At last, Olivia sensed a shift in Chase. An acquiescence.

She leaned forward. "What should I wear to lunch?"

EIGHT

Despite his qualms, Chase sent a car and driver to pick Olivia up on Tuesday and bring her to Al-Ain, a Palestinian restaurant south of Capitol Hill, near the Navy Yard neighborhood.

Olivia carefully dressed in a long, flowing skirt, demure long-sleeved blouse, and headscarf designed to put Mousa and any other patrons of the restaurant at ease—while simultaneously allowing her to conceal a weapon in a thigh holster. In a small purse worn across her body, she'd tucked a set of lockpick tools. The large boho pendant concealed a small camera. And Julia had remotely activated her cellphone's microphone to transmit without the phone being on.

For the first time on the mission, Olivia felt a thrum of nervous fear. She reminded herself that it was highly unlikely that Mousa would suspect her of being a CIA officer, let alone abduct her in broad daylight in D.C.

Monica and Julia had also taken up positions not far from the restaurant, which catered to an upscale crowd with its fusion of Mediterranean cuisine. Monica, Alpha Team's sniper, had overwatch from the low roof of the office building across the street. Julia sat in the coffee shop on the street level, her laptop and earbuds along with her nondescript gray hoodie and leggings suggesting student or writer. She, however, had a secure browser open to run intel through classified databases and a 9mm gun in her backpack.

Chase met Olivia outside the entrance. He looked tired, and when he smiled, it didn't quite light his eyes as it always had. He took her hand, leaning in to kiss her. Olivia, who'd expected this show, nevertheless caught her breath and melted into it. Their nerves and the chemistry between them turned into an authentic romantic expression.

When Chase leaned back, the strain around his eyes had eased.

Taking her hand, he led her into the lion's den.

Mousa, a dark-haired man with a beard and broad shoulders, stood as the host led them to the large round table in the back corner where he sat with two other dark-haired men, who also stood.

"Chase! My brother!" said Mousa, his voice booming as he clasped Chase's hand and pulled him into a hug before kissing Chase on both cheeks.

The other men smiled and shook Chase's hand as they all murmured the traditional greeting '*Assalaam 'alaikum*' to which Chase responded, '*Wa 'alaikum assalaam.*' Mousa introduced them as his associates.

Olivia waited until the men turned and greeted her with *May peace be upon you* in Arabic. Pressing her hand over her heart, she dipped her chin and responded with *and peace be upon you*, also in Arabic.

As she did, she prayed that Julia had received clear images of Mousa's 'associates.'

Mousa smiled. "Ah, you grace us with your kindness, Ms. Markham. After your experience in Ibiza, to honor our traditions and speak our language—it shows a true nobility of spirit." He gestured toward the table. "Please, sit here next to me. I hope to learn more about you over lunch."

Olivia refrained from glancing at Chase, who'd stiffened next to her before putting his hand possessively on her lower back. Truthfully, she'd wondered how quickly Mousa would get to her surviving the Ibiza *jihadis*, but now that he had, she had a better handle on her own approach.

She shrugged. "I try not to stereotype others, Mr. Mousa. I wouldn't want other people to see me as an airhead and frivolous party girl just because I'm blond and in college."

But, of course, she knew full well that by describing herself that way she reinforced Mousa's view of her.

Or so she hoped.

If Mousa saw anything more than what she wanted him to see, at best she'd lose her chance to get closer to real intel.

At worst, Mousa might just accomplish what the *jihadi* who'd stabbed her hadn't.

Mousa had already ordered for the table. Multiple platters of colorful dishes intended for communal dining came almost as soon as she and Chase took their seats. Chase had already warned her that no business would be discussed prior to the meal, which, as it was midday, would be large.

What neither had expected was Mousa's probing questions of Olivia as they ate. He wanted to know everything about her. Uneasy, Olivia told him as much as she felt comfortable sharing, though she wasn't sure that she should say anything about her parents and brother and sister. Her intuition told her to minimize her relationship with them, saying truthfully that her parents didn't know why she'd moved to Bethesda and taken up her music studies again.

Mousa, dipping some fluffy pita into a plate of mushroom hummus, took a large bite. He gestured with the remaining pita as he said while chewing, "If you were my daughter, *abna*, I would not let you go anywhere so far from me. The world, as you know, can be a very brutal place."

A creeping sensation crawled down Olivia's back. Her medal, hidden under her blouse, warmed against her skin. She swallowed.

That felt like an implied threat.

She picked up her water glass and sipped. Chase, who'd sat tense and barely eating, slipped a hand onto her thigh. Olivia laid her own on top of his. In response, he twisted his fingers and entwined them with hers. His pulse tapped against her wrist, but his palm remained warm and dry.

At last Olivia agreed with Mousa's statement as if it were a benign observation. "That's true," she said, "but fortunately you're not my father, and the world is also filled with so many amazing things to experience. For example, I can enjoy your company and this delicious food."

Mousa laughed before waving his hand at a waiting server, who brought him a glass of red wine. Olivia knew that strict observance forbade Muslims from drinking alcohol, but she also knew that many did in private and away from the censorious gaze of religious leaders.

"Well, then Chase must bring you with him when he comes to Macau," said Mousa, turning back to his plate.

Chase, who'd just taken a bite of food, choked. Coughing, he reached for his water glass. The other two men, who'd said little during the meal, looked at each other. Olivia's senses buzzed. She waited, however. It wouldn't be proper for her to speak about the trip or Chase's plans.

"Macau?" asked Chase, blinking as if coming into bright sunlight from the dark interior of a building. "Why would I travel to Macau?"

Mousa smiled and reached for a platter of molded rice with spiced lamb and eggplant that he'd told Olivia was called *maqluba*. "Because that is where you will set up accounts for us." He looked up and caught Olivia's gaze with his. "But what am I saying? This is too boring for Olivia. Investment banking makes *me* want to take a nap. You must be ready to cry. We will not speak of this again. I will call you later, brother, to finalize details."

The rest of lunch passed without another word about investments or Olivia's background. Instead, she and Chase described the upcoming Strathmore concert featuring their duet to Mousa and his silent tablemates. Mousa promised to attend and donate a large sum to the AIR program in their honor. The other men, Tarek and Wael, said nothing about either the concert or the donation. They seemed less like guests and more like bodyguards to Olivia. No one left the table during the meal. As far as Olivia could tell, no intel, coded or physical, passed between the Palestinians and Chase.

Olivia wondered if she'd failed again.

Until Starling showed up later that afternoon at the secure location where Sam had called a combined team meeting.

Olivia hadn't seen Starling since Germany or talked to him since their phone negotiations in June. She suspected that Starling kept close tabs on her beyond the status reports that she knew Sam provided.

She'd forgotten how hard Starling's eyes were.

"Markham," he said, briefly dipping his chin toward her before addressing the team. "Good work, everyone. That's the first time we've had a lead on where the money will go offshore. And thanks to Markham and Hendricks, we now have identities of two key players in the network. Tarek El Shaer and Wael Khatib are commanders in the Black Hand, an elite unit within the military arm of Hamas."

Julia followed this weighty revelation with the question that had hummed at the back of Olivia's thoughts all afternoon, ever since Mousa had made it clear that Chase needed to bring her to the autonomous Chinese city-state known as the Las Vegas of Asia.

"Sir, why Macau? Al Rahji Bank opened a Malaysian branch two years ago. Wouldn't that be a better choice?"

Al Rahji Bank, a Saudi bank used by one of the 9-11 terrorists to launder hundreds of thousands of dollars, had long been suspected by the CIA as knowingly supporting terrorism.

Starling shook his head. "No. Operation Green Quest taught us that these terrorists are very good at masking what they do through layering. Besides, Al Rahji maintains plausible deniability and wouldn't welcome an explicit link with the Black Hand."

"Macau makes perfect sense, actually," said Tess. "The monetary border is pretty porous if you know what you're doing. It's a miracle Macau hasn't made it to the FATF's watchlists, not even the grey list."

The Financial Action Task Force, an intergovernmental watchdog monitoring global money laundering and terrorist financing, comprised dozens of countries. Located in Paris, FATF issued guidance three times a year on those countries that failed to protect the international financial system. High-risk countries appeared on the black list; countries with increased monitoring who actively worked with the FATF to fix their problems made it on the grey list.

Starling returned to Olivia. "Markham, you'll need to stay sharp. The Chinese have been extremely active lately. Assume you're being watched. Someone may approach you, including Chase, especially if they see him meeting with Saudi arms brokers."

Yet another potential landmine in the operation. The headache that had started at lunch moved down Olivia's neck and into her shoulders.

"Abadi left Marseille this morning booked on a flight to Istanbul. We'll pick him up there. We're one step closer to stopping the sale, but more importantly, getting inside Hamas's financing network. We need the names of the people linking legitimate banks with the terrorists' *hawaladar* network."

Hawaladar were trusted money brokers that operated outside of—and sometimes in parallel to—traditional banks. *Hawala* systems relied on trust and honor between brokers, who kept informal tallies of debt. No money was sent directly between parties, and tracing transactions was nearly impossible.

Starling had just moved the mission goalposts. *A lot.* Olivia was beginning to understand that often happened on covert operations.

He left shortly after that.

Then Sam assigned Tess and Fiona to surveil El Shaer and Khatib, who'd flown into the U.S. the previous week under false identities. Julia, who now had Chase's Blackberry number, headed out to implement a software wiretap on the phone service before going through the transcript of the audio recorded during lunch and images of restaurant staff captured by Olivia's covert camera. Monica and Tara left to begin preparing for Alpha Team's upcoming trip to Macau.

After the other team members had gone, Sam turned to Olivia. She thought she saw concern in his gray eyes, but it disappeared too quickly to be sure.

"Markham, my contacts in Clandestine Services tell me that the SSSB recently recruited an American college student in Shanghai and paid him to apply to the CIA." He paused before asking, "How vulnerable is Chase to blackmail?"

Olivia hadn't considered that aspect from Starling's warning. She'd assumed he meant that Chase appeared open to working with known enemies of the United States.

"I don't know," she said honestly. "I can brush up on Mandarin, especially the dialect spoken in Shanghai, and keep my ears open. I can also make sure he's never approachable."

Sam nodded, the cloud returning to his gaze. "I'm sorry to add bodyguard to your mission, but we know almost nothing about how Chinese intelligence works, especially the Shanghai branch which doesn't send its top officers on to the CCP. Just be extra careful that you don't give away your language fluency or Agency connections or you'll become the target."

Although the teams remained on alert for the mission to Macau, Olivia had to wait until Thursday before Chase contacted her for a rehearsal.

When she arrived at his house, he met her at the door with a moody expression and a drink in one hand. He handed her a handwritten note with travel details—flight date, hotel, and instructions that included packing evening gowns supplied by one of the charities that he ran. It turned out that the designer dresses were heavily adorned with costly gems that could be mistaken for cut-glass costume jewelry.

That was how the terrorists would transfer the bulk of their funds.

That and the actual jewelry collection fit for a Saudi princess that Olivia would wear with the gowns, which Chase surprised her with once they'd arrived in Macau. While he would meet with banking officials to set up legitimate accounts on behalf of ISNA, funded by their earnings from the private equity fund he managed, he would also pay the Saudi arms dealer with the jewelry. In turn, Abadi would sell it and deposit the funds in Al Rahji Malaysia.

Mousa had turned a survivor of a *jihadi* attack into a Hamas mule. Olivia, already eager to subvert Mousa's plans, burned at the insult.

She was *so* going to enjoy the results of the poison pill that Chase would deliver along with the new bank accounts in Macau.

Chase had booked them a villa at the MGM Macau, overlooking the South China Sea. The opulent hotel and casino initially overwhelmed Olivia, who'd never been to Vegas. She wondered how Monica and Julia, who'd booked a guest room, would manage to keep track of them beyond the GPS transmitter that she wore in a hair clip. She'd been forced to leave her St. Michael medal in the villa safe, and despite the heavy necklace, bracelets, and earrings she wore, felt naked without the modest pewter disc.

Their first night in Macau was for show. Mousa had warned Chase that Abadi would contact him for an in-person meet, but that in the meantime, they should 'enjoy' themselves eating in one of the three-star Michelin restaurants—perhaps at Aux Beaux Arts, which would remind them of their impromptu Parisian date.

Olivia shivered, glancing around the busy hotel lobby as she and Chase walked to dinner, and touched the heavy diamond teardrop at her throat.

Mousa had likely sent someone to watch them.

The next day, Chase had a meeting at Citibank Macau, where he had an appointment with an investment manager in private banking services. To launder money going to terrorists, he would set up a series of linked accounts leading to a final account associated with an Indonesian Muslim charity for widows and orphans.

It was a fake charity.

But in setting up the accounts, Chase would give administrative access to a non-existent Graham Investments subsidiary fund. A fund that Julia managed for the CIA. After Chase left Macau, Julia would return to Citibank, brandish her false credentials, and then access the accounts. From there, all account transactions would be tagged and traced.

Olivia, mindful of her dual role as bodyguard, escorted Chase to Citibank. Her neck tingled as they approached the entrance to the bank.

"Kiss me," she said to Chase, following the command with a tug on his hand.

He turned, a slight frown marring his handsome face. Before he could say anything, Olivia rose and wound her arms around his neck. Chase pulled her against him. And for a moment, Olivia forgot that she was a novice intelligence officer in a large foreign city being followed by hostile actors.

Perhaps it was the heightened danger they both felt. Certainly they'd ignored the growing chemistry between them. Whatever it was, Olivia's heart raced and her head swam as Chase's lips caressed hers.

When at last he pulled back and leaned his forehead against hers, they were both panting.

"It's going to be okay," she said.

"I know." He didn't sound convinced. "I'll text you when it's done."

As she strolled away, Olivia kept watch in the large windows next to her. A dark-haired man followed fifty meters behind carrying a shopping bag.

Abadi.

She ducked into a clothing store and waited.

Five minutes later, the Saudi arms dealer entered, scanning the interior. Olivia had stationed herself facing out and near the front where Abadi couldn't trap her. She'd noted the rear door but couldn't count on escape that way. She hoped that Monica, her shadow, would let this play out before following Abadi into the store.

He stopped at a rack across from her, glancing in her direction as he set the shopping bag down. His dark eyes were fathomless. He nodded once and then circled the rack of clothes before heading outside again.

Olivia, her heart tapping like a wounded sparrow at her ribcage, waited a minute before pulling a dress from the rack and approaching the package to recover it. Then she made her way to the counter where a salesclerk rang up her sale. She slipped Abadi's bag into the new bag and left the store.

As she walked away, the sense of being observed returned, stronger than ever. She watched store windows, crossed the street in unpredictable intervals, entered buildings suddenly, and doubled back more than once. But none of the techniques she'd learned for discerning a tail succeeded. Whoever it was was very good.

Forty-five minutes later, Chase texted. *It's done.*

Olivia waited until they achieved the relative security of the villa before telling Chase about the surprise drop.

Inside Abadi's bag was a poker chip from the Wynn Macau and a table number. The hands of a Rolex still in its box pointed to nine. A flyer in Cantonese described a local pawn shop where the gems from the dresses could be exchanged for local currency.

The meet was set.

Chase went to the minibar and pulled out a couple of bottles of vodka along with a soda. Olivia watched him mix a strong drink.

"He won't discover anything unusual about the jewelry," she said, her eyes narrowed as Chase drank deeply. "Delivering it is the last part of our task. Others will deal with Abadi and Kader. Nothing will get back to Mousa tying to you."

"I just want this over with. I want my life back."

Olivia came over and took the empty tumbler from his hand. "That's going to take a little longer as you know. But I'll be with you every step of the way. I promise."

Their gazes met. Desire flared, hot and white as phosphorous.

Chase raised a fingertip and stroked Olivia's cheek. Then, cupping her jaw, he leaned down and kissed her. Vodka and passion tangled as he thrust his tongue into her eager mouth.

Olivia moaned, pressing into his hard chest. Her nipples tightened, and electricity hummed along her skin.

Chase pulled back. "I want you, Olivia, more than I ever wanted anyone. Let me make love to you."

A muffled warning bell sounded in the far reaches of Olivia's mind. She should stop and assess the situation.

Instead, she rose onto her toes and kissed Chase, twining her fingers in his hair.

He responded by growling and picking her up before carrying her across the villa and to his bedroom.

NINE

At nine that night, Chase sat at a poker table in the high-limit area of the Wynn Macau with Olivia at his shoulder wearing the jewelry. They had used the cash from the costly dress ornamentation to buy-in with the dealer, who would take a cut for his role in the deal with Abadi, arriving later. Although Macau had an environment to rival Las Vegas, it was still early days in the city-state's foray into gambling, meaning that it was easy to get into a high-stakes game and easy for professional players to win big.

The red evening gown that Olivia wore, the one that Mousa had picked for the meet with Abadi, bit into her flesh along all its edges, including the diamond-shaped opening on her torso and the heavy halter strap that twined around her neck. The material, encrusted with tiny opaque discs and metallic sequins on both sides, lacked a lining so that it rubbed Olivia's skin as she moved.

It was like wearing coarse sandpaper.

The constant irritation had started to drive Olivia a little mad. She thought that numerous hostile gazes watched them, especially her.

They sat in a quieter area of the casino, one where serious poker players could concentrate on the game, and yet she could identify no source for the feeling of imminent threat.

She raised her fingertip in unconscious habit to her chest, but it only connected with the heavy, soulless diamond.

Abadi had directed them to a Texas Hold'em table with no limit on betting where ten players sat around the dealer. He wasn't there, however.

Olivia took a dainty sip from her rose-and-gin cocktail. Rose petals swirled around the colorless liquid, which was more gin than syrup in keeping with the casino's goal of intoxicating the players and their companions. She couldn't afford to drink on the job, but the romantic concoction had appealed to her.

As a server moved by her, Olivia set the still-full drink on her tray. Another would appear within a few minutes.

Her gaze connected with a beautiful Chinese woman wearing a midnight-blue evening gown cut in a deep-V to her waist and embellished with silver embroidery and sequins.

The woman dipped her chin graciously, her smoky-gray eyeshadow and graceful movements adding a sense of mystery and nobility.

Olivia's internal antennae quivered, but she nodded before turning back to the poker table.

Abadi showed up around midnight, after Chase had won a substantial amount of money. The table had attracted a growing body of spectators who stood in respectful silence around the players. Olivia wondered how the hand-off would happen.

Abadi waited until the man next to Chase cashed out before nodding at the dealer and taking his seat. Chase pushed away from the table before the dealer had finished accepting Abadi's buy-in. He left his chips stacked, however, signaling an intention to return. Olivia followed him from the tables and beyond into the busy hotel lobby. Tension radiated from him.

He headed toward the hotel gift shop, Olivia at his side.

Invisible fingers of alarm kneaded Olivia's spine. Taking Chase's arm, she glanced around but saw no one watching them. Looking up, she scanned Chase's flattened lips and his tight jaw muscles. Under her fingers and next to her side, he'd turned to wood.

In the gift shop, Chase made a show of looking over the jewelry inside a locked case. Then he bought Olivia a matching set of gold earrings, necklace, and bracelet studded with tiny, inexpensive sapphires. On a whim, he also bought her a bottle of Ralph Lauren *Romance*, saying it reminded him of their trip to Paris. It also provided Olivia with another bag with which to hide the smaller bag of jewelry.

Without speaking, Olivia accepted both giftbags and walked with Chase to the nearby restrooms, where she changed the more expensive jewelry she wore for the cheaper pieces, carefully nestling them inside the giftshop boxes. It would be up to Olivia to handle the delivery of the package to Abadi.

Knowing that she might not get another chance for some time, she used the facilities and touched up her makeup. When she came out of the restroom, she found Chase talking to the stunning Chinese woman.

A jolt of jealousy and fear hit her. She'd promised to make sure that no one could approach Chase, let alone another woman so compelling she drew all gazes.

Olivia smoothed the frown from her brow and joined them, sliding next to Chase, who wrapped an arm around her.

The other woman looked at her. "Good evening. I was just saying to your friend that he should not have left the table when he did. He gave position to the new player on the right."

Her English, spoken with a British accent, was flawless. Olivia detected a slight exotic timbre that signaled her native language. Some slight tonal variation suggested it wasn't Mandarin. Perhaps Cantonese, more dominant in Macau and Hong Kong, where many locals spoke British English.

Olivia decided to play to stereotype. Smiling broadly, she said with a Texas accent, "See, Sweetheart, I told you I could wait to use the toilet. We'd better hurry back to the table before your luck changes on you."

She pivoted, pulling Chase along with her.

The Chinese woman caused a hitch in her step, however, when she called after them, "Your new necklace brings out the color of your eyes, but the other pendant has more elegance."

Olivia tossed a glance behind her, her smile fairly cracking her cheeks. Letting her words slur, she said the first thing that occurred to her. "Oh, that old thing? Daddy would kill me if he knew I took it to pay a gambling debt."

Then they returned to the poker table.

Olivia accepted a drink from a server and moved to stand between Chase and Abadi, who ignored their return. She sipped from the drink, this time addressing Chase a little loudly, especially given the otherwise quiet space around the table, whose players had rotated over the three hours into a serious, skilled bunch.

But Olivia needed to set up the pass.

Laying a hand on Chase's shoulder, she leaned closer and pretended to stage whisper into his ear. The kind of whisper a foolish, inebriated young woman would make when she was trying to be quiet and failing.

"Darlin', discard that ol' one-eyed Jack," she said, pointing a shaky forefinger at Chase's hand.

There was no one-eyed Jack, of course. But as Chase, who had no idea what play Olivia intended, looked up at her with narrowed eyes, Olivia tipped her full cocktail, held out beside her, over Abadi.

Who proceeded to let out an explosive shout and stand.

Olivia apologized profusely, swiping at Abadi with her free hand. As he danced away from her overeager ministrations, she deftly slipped the smaller jewelry bag into his seat.

Minor mayhem occurred as a server came to help clean Abadi and the table. Murmuring rose around the standing spectators, but all of the poker players watched with expressionless faces. Some held their hands as before. One or two laid their cards on the green felt and leaned back, arms crossed.

After Abadi settled back into his seat, the casino floor manager tapped Olivia on the shoulder and asked her to come with him. Chase began to stand to go with them, but the Chinese woman stepped in and urged Chase to continue playing. A discreet casino security guard in a tailored black suit watched from ten meters away. Olivia knew that he would only step in if she became disruptive, however.

She could see no way out of being separated from Chase, so for the time being she let the floor manager, a slight middle-aged man whose soft voice conveyed firm regret, lead her away from the high-limit area.

Olivia found herself escorted to a quiet bar available to big spenders where a server brought her coffee and pastry. Alarm had started to shriek through her, making her head pound. Her little "oopsie" scarcely merited this treatment. She suspected that the Chinese woman had somehow orchestrated her removal from Chase's side.

She texted Monica as soon as she was alone. *Do you have eyes on the asset?*

Affirmative. He's still playing poker. But he's got some new eye candy in blue who's giving me the willies. Get back as soon as you can.

Copy that. My radar pinged the Blue Widow right away.

Hold up. The Blue Widow just left, but a male with a thousand-yard stare shifted closer to the table. My gut tells me he's the babysitter.

Where had the Chinese operative gone? Olivia had to get back to Chase and get him out of the casino. She waited until the floor manager departed and then headed for the exit.

Where she was stopped by none other than the Chinese Blue Widow.

"Please, Ms. Markham," said the woman, gesturing back into the bar, "indulge me with some of your time."

Ms. Markham. She knew that Olivia wasn't the ditzy wealthy Texan daughter she'd portrayed earlier. What did she make of Olivia's act? Olivia would know soon enough if the Blue Widow suspected her of anything besides being a college student far from home.

"Of course," she said without the accent or slurred speech.

The Chinese Blue Widow fell into stride with her. As they passed by a large mirror, Olivia couldn't help taking in their striking contrast: she with her long pale blond hair and formfitting, bright-red gown, the other woman with black hair gleaming in a smooth chignon, her silky midnight-blue gown floating behind her.

The odd sensation of being out of her depth and alone in a foreign country passed through Olivia like a sonic boom.

She sat at the table with her untouched coffee and pastry. The other woman sat across from her, crossing her legs. A server came with a white porcelain pot and two small cups. She poured them each steaming tea, cleared the coffee and pastry, then bowed and left.

Olivia waited for the other woman to pick up her fragrant brew.

Then the Blue Widow smiled at her. "I am Liú Xiù. Do not worry about your friend. He has recovered all that he lost when he gave up position."

Some hidden meaning freighted her words, but Olivia knew better than to ask directly.

She shrugged, letting the breath she held out with the movement. "For now. But I'm his good luck charm. I should return to his side."

Liú Xiù tilted her head, studying Olivia. "I wonder how well you know your friend?"

Olivia's breath caught before she could stop it. "Well enough," she said.

Liú Xiù kept her steady gaze on Olivia for a long moment. Olivia didn't rise to the bait, instead breathing as *Sensei* Mark always reminded her when facing a formidable sparring opponent. She raised her teacup and swallowed a mouthful. It helped.

"Do you know that the Central Intelligence Agency of your government has you under surveillance?" asked the other woman at last.

"What?" asked Olivia, alarm sharpening her tone. Even as her thoughts whirled, a small voice told her that her alarm was natural for a naïve young college student.

Liú Xiù nodded at someone. A moment later, a male in a suit handed Olivia a manila envelope. He stepped to the side of the table and crossed his hands in the stance of bodyguards everywhere.

"Open it. There you will see an American female following you and your friend everywhere in Macau."

Olivia, her fingers shaking a little despite herself, opened the flap and pulled a stack of glossy photos from the envelope. She expected to see Monica or Julia, but instead a familiar blonde appeared.

For a moment, she sat with a blank expression trying to process what she saw.

Fortunately, Liú Xiù seemed to misinterpret Olivia's lack of comprehension.

"This woman arrived here before you and Mr. Graham. She has been very interested in what you are doing. Perhaps it is the company you keep."

As she said this, Olivia came to a photo showing Abadi leaving the clothing store followed by another image of her walking out after him.

"I don't understand," said Olivia, stalling for time.

"That is Saad Abadi, a Saudi Arabian arms dealer," said Liú Xiù. "He sits next to Mr. Graham even now."

"Who are you? Why are you telling me this?" asked Olivia, licking her dry lips. Her head ached as though it would split open any moment.

Liú Xiù sipped her tea and, setting it down, smiled. "I? I am someone who would be your friend. I understand how easy it is to be led astray by feelings of love—and passion, never forget that—and overlook little signs that a lover is involved in something ... unsavory, shall I say?"

Olivia had no idea what to say to this, except to continue to play dumb. "Are you saying that Chase is somehow mixed up with this ... Saad Abadi?" She deliberately said the name with uncertainty and a New England accent.

Liú Xiù reached for the teapot and poured them each more tea. "Let me offer you some advice, Ms. Markham. Do not worry about Mr. Abadi. Or the jewelry that Mr. Graham asked you to give him. I suggest that you focus on enjoying the rest of your stay here in Macau. The MGM has a fabulous spa. You should also try shopping on the Grande Praça instead of near the Citibank office."

In other words, I know where you're staying and where you've been. Don't stray where you're not wanted.

Or where I have to find you.

Olivia drank her tea as if considering the other woman's words before nodding politely. "Thank you, Ms. Liú." She remembered in time to mangle the Mandarin pronunciation of her interlocuter's name. "I'll take your kind advice. Now, if you'll excuse me, I'll return to Chase. I really am his lucky charm."

Liú Xiù inclined her head.

Olivia stood as the bodyguard stepped forward. *Ah, an armed escort. Charming.*

Watch her and the male closely, said Liú Xiù to the escort in Mandarin. *She knows more than she's saying.*

The enigmatic Chinese spy hadn't bought Olivia's clumsy attempt at subterfuge.

Tension spiked in Olivia's chest.

As they returned to the poker game, Olivia caught sight of the back of a familiar tall blonde in a pewter evening gown covered in sequins. She headed away from them in the nearly empty hall. She'd obviously not timed Olivia's meeting with the intimidating SSSB agent well or Olivia would never have seen her.

When she arrived at Chase's side, her escort disappeared in the crowd of silent spectators surrounding the poker table. But Olivia knew now the dual sources of her profound sense of being watched. There were at least two male SSSB agents in the room. And Crane was somewhere in the hotel.

She texted Monica again. *We need to clear out now. Alert Juicy Fruit to pack up. Go your separate ways. Stay sharp. I picked up eyes ... including a crane kicked from the Nest.*

Affirmative. Be seeing you.

Monica and Julia would travel individually to Hong Kong where they would then fly on two separate commercial flights back to the U.S. Olivia and Chase, who'd flown by private helicopter from the former British colony, would have to find their own way home.

Olivia bent and spoke into Chase's ear. "Time to fold, darlin'."

Chase stiffened but dipped his chin in acknowledgement.

Abadi, who still played in the cut-out position, ignored their departure. Olivia didn't spare him a glance. They'd delivered the package per her mission objective, and now her objective was to get the asset back to the U.S. safely. What did or didn't happen with the Saudi arms dealer and the purchase of SAMs by a Hamas-affiliated terror group was no longer her concern.

"We have a tail," she said to Chase, smiling as she slipped her arm into his before they set off into the still-crowded casino. "Chinese intelligence has been watching us. They know about the payment to Abadi."

To his credit, Chase only glanced down at her and smiled back. But his green eyes had widened. "What does that mean?"

"I don't know yet," she said, guiding him with pressure on his arm toward a mass of drunken tourists where one of them had just won a large payout. She used the direction change to confirm that the two male SSSB agents still followed. "We need to get out of Macau without being seen."

"That's easier said than done. The fastest way off the island is private helicopter, but we'll never get one this time of night. We'd need to wait until ten tomorrow morning. And we'd have to go to the ferry terminal anyway."

"Then let's distract the babysitters in the meantime." Olivia grabbed a drink from a tray of cocktails being served to the cheering gamblers. "Who won?"

A large, sweaty-faced man in shirtsleeves and crumpled slacks looked at her.

"I did! Looks like I won again," he said as Olivia came closer and raised her drink to him. He grabbed her and pulled her into his arms, twirling her.

Olivia and Chase stayed with the tourists until the wee hours, buying them drinks and encouraging rowdiness and gambling. Neither Olivia nor Chase drank anything, surreptitiously switching their cups with the other drinkers. Olivia managed to get a large sweatshirt from one of the men, Brits on holiday, and dragged it over her head while Chase blocked the view. Then she repeated her earlier oopsie, this time in a much more flamboyant manner in which she staggered into a server with a full tray of drinks.

The tourists began to career around, knocking into other gamblers like drunken cue balls. Thirty seconds afterwards, a team of casino security guards rushed in to break up the inevitable brawl.

Olivia slipped off her heels, grabbed Chase by the hand, and hurried to the elevators. They needed to get to their room and grab their passports and her go bag. As the elevator door slid shut, Olivia saw both SSSB agents wading into the drunken fray.

Good. They wouldn't realize that Olivia and Chase had left for several minutes.

Ten minutes later, Olivia wore yoga pants, T-shirt, and the purloined sweatshirt. She wished she had a handgun to tuck into an ankle holster. But flying commercial had its limitations. And a gun definitely removed all doubt about her bystander role. Chase had changed into a pair of worn jeans, faded denim jacket, sneakers, and ballcap. They looked as nondescript as possible.

They managed to get out of the MGM unseen, but Olivia knew it was a race against time and there were only so many places they could run. By now, the SSSB likely watched both ferry terminals and the international airport in Macau.

They grabbed a cab to the Venetian Hotel on the Cotai peninsula, the world's largest casino and sure to be packed even at this hour. Olivia wanted to get lost in the crowds there. They would also buy new clothes, changing a second time. Olivia waited until they'd made it to the dimly lit interior of the replica of Italy's famous lagoon-surrounded city to call Sam.

His phone number had been disconnected.

Sharp unease creeping down her spine, Olivia tried Tess, then Tara, and finally Fiona, who answered.

"Not on this line. I'll call you back at that number. Standby."

Cold dread pooled in Olivia's stomach. Something was terribly wrong.

Two minutes passed before Fiona called back.

"Sam's been disavowed," she said without preamble. "Supposedly he set up some accounts in the Bahamas where he sent payments to people who only exist on paper. Starling brought a team to the secure location and tore it apart. Sam's in the wind."

Disbelief and anger burned off the dread. "That's utter bullshit!" said Olivia. "Starling's the one running ghost assets. I have the proof."

"Doesn't matter. You're in Macau. Bravo Team was ordered to come in to debrief. Tess and Tara are at Langley now. It stinks, so I waited for you to check in to let you know. Alpha Team is on its own."

Olivia, who'd been scanning the concourse they walked through, pulled Chase into the next dark alcove. "Take my advice and disappear."

"Already on my way," said Fiona. "Get a burner and text me at this number in twenty-four hours."

"Wilco," said Olivia.

"And Olivia? I get the feeling Starling has something special in mind for you. Watch your back."

TEN

Fiona's warning was terrifyingly accurate. Starling's "something special" had followed them into the Venetian Macau.

Olivia's nerves buzzed as she stared across the concourse of the Grand Canal Shoppes at the tall blonde twenty meters behind them.

Lily Crane.

How the hell had she found them in the crowds at the Venetian Macau?

A few weeks ago, during the Mid-Autumn Festival, and the crush of visitors from mainland China would have made surveillance and tracking impossible. As it was, finding them among throngs of tourists shopping at more than 300 boutiques should have been more than a single field operative could manage on her own.

Unless she'd planted a tracking device on her targets. Or had a team. Or both.

Crap. They couldn't afford to stop and go through their clothes now. And she'd just have to pray that Lily didn't have any partners.

Lily wouldn't wait until Olivia had gotten stateside to deliver whatever it was that Starling had in mind. Olivia knew it, just as sure as she knew that the other woman held a grudge against her for getting kicked off the team.

The mission had just gone sideways and straight off the pages of the CIA playbook and into the realm of nightmares.

Olivia looked at Chase. "We're being followed."

"Not the Chinese I take it," he said, his voice steady. He'd proven remarkably steely, all things considered.

She shook her head. As she spoke, she saw Lily stop a few meters past their position and backtrack. "I can't explain now. Just follow my lead."

Olivia pulled Chase through the shoppers crowding the concourse, glancing back over her shoulder.

Lily had caught the scent. Their gazes clashed. Lily's eyes narrowed, clear hostility sparking in her gaze. She began pushing through the people around her, many of whom loudly complained.

Olivia didn't see any other "tourists" change course as she and Chase wove their way toward the outside entrance, but there was just no time to scan and assess. They had to put distance between them and Lily so that Olivia could search for the tracker.

Up ahead, Olivia recognized the uniform of high-end security personnel the world over: a discreet black jacket and a wired earpiece. She veered through the crowd, which parted around her and Chase as a river moves around a boulder, and came to a halt in front of the security officer.

"Sir, sir," she said in Mandarin, "that woman tried to take my bag!" She pointed toward Lily, who drew up short as the guard's gaze swiveled toward her.

Then Lily pivoted and headed away from them, not running but moving quickly.

The security officer nodded, said, "I see her. Stay here," in Mandarin, and took off after Lily. Olivia heard him calling for backup.

Once the crowd had swallowed the security officer, Olivia immediately tugged Chase to continue racing toward the exit. Once outside, she hailed a taxi. She had no idea what to do next, except to tell the driver to head toward one of the tourist sites farther west, so that she could go through their possessions as best she could in the back seat.

"Largo do Senado,' she said, pronouncing the words as a native speaker would.

The historic center of Macau, Senado Square drew tourists. The alleys pinwheeling from the square and open only to pedestrian traffic, featured food stands and clothing stores along walking routes to other historic sites. Perhaps not the Venetian, but it would be hard to track them, provided she could find whatever Lily had planted.

Olivia twisted toward Chase. She spoke in French. There was no need for the taxi driver to follow their conversation or identify them as American. "Finding us at the Venetian was like finding a needle in a haystack. I'm going to look for a tracker. Take off your jacket."

She took the hat he wore while he maneuvered in the confined space to remove his denim jacket. By the time they'd reached Senado Square, Olivia had found a tiny square electronic device inside the lining of the pocket. She told Chase to leave the jacket.

The driver let Chase and Olivia out south of the 18th-Century landmark, which was inaptly named 'square' in Portuguese. Instead, the massive plaza, paved with black-and-white stones set in an alternating wave pattern and surrounded by pastel neoclassical architecture, resembled an elongated teardrop.

As they hustled across the street toward the square, Olivia scanned the closest buildings, not at all sure what she was looking for.

Ah ha! There.

A couple of hundred meters from the street and just northeast of the large round fountain in the middle of the teardrop stood a large white building with the words *Santa Casa Da Misericórdia* written in black beneath the pediment. It was the only building within sight that didn't have numerous tourists milling around its arcaded façade or obvious shops.

"Let's go!" Olivia took Chase by the hand and hustled him toward the entrance.

Inside they were greeted with a UNESCO-heritage-site museum. Olivia paid the nominal entrance fee. Then they found the restrooms so that she could examine her own clothing. There was no way that Lily had planted only one tracker.

In this, she was correct.

Another tracker had been slipped into the lining of her backpack, which she used as a go bag.

Olivia cut the tracker out and left it on the back of the toilet in the stall where she'd undressed before tugging her clothing and shoes back on. When she emerged, Chase leaned against a sink, arms crossed and eyes shadowed.

"What's going on, Olivia?" he asked. There was an edge to his voice. "Are you really with the CIA? Or did you lie to me?"

Stunned, Olivia blinked, and her chin dropped.

A moment later, the door to the restroom opened, and Lily Crane walked in, gripping a 9mm handgun with two hands.

"Oh, she's with the Company all right," said Lily, grinning at Chase. "We trained together." She looked at Olivia. "Hi, roomie. Miss me?"

Olivia's heart banged against her chest, and her mouth and throat dried. However, she crossed her arms and adopted a casual stance—as casual as one could be, trapped in a museum restroom with a suddenly hostile asset and a gun-wielding nemesis.

"Now that you ask, let me think about it." She tilted her head and touched her fingertip to her lips in a mockery of consideration. "Um, no. No, I can't say I do."

Lily laughed. The grating sound bounced off the white tile before stabbing Olivia's eardrums. "Well, that's just too bad. I came halfway around the world to surprise you. I guess I won't expect any appreciation for my efforts then." The grin dropped from her face as she gripped Chase's upper arm while ramming the gun muzzle into his side. "Let's go. I need to stage your deaths."

Olivia had known Starling was a bastard, but she'd never figured him for a murderer. "Straying from the mission objective, Crane?" she guessed, forcing herself to inject humor that she didn't feel into her voice. "Are you sure Starling will be okay with you making your own play? If not, you're a bigger fool than I thought you were. And that's saying something."

She didn't look at Chase, afraid of what she'd see in his face.

Afraid that she wouldn't be able to do or say whatever she needed as a field intelligence officer in a life-or-death situation.

As Olivia had intended, Lily growled. What she hadn't intended was Lily pistol-whipping Chase. He grunted and bent forward, catching himself on the doorframe to the restroom before he collapsed to the floor.

Lily glared at Olivia as Chase retched and threw up, managing to miss the other operative's shoes.

"You say something, I strike him. Get that, Princess Barbie?" she asked. "You don't have your relic white knight here to step in and save your candy ass. I suggest you come along meekly or there will be others not so closely involved in our little drama who'll suffer."

After she said this, she pushed the door open a few inches. In the hallway outside the restroom was a mother with a small child and a baby in a stroller. Shielding her Glock behind the door, Lily smiled at the little girl, "Hi, Sweetness. How're you enjoying your visit to the museum? Too many dumb porcelain vases, am I right?"

The little girl, perhaps sensing something off with the big blond woman, gripped her mother's leg and ducked her head.

The distracted mother snapped at the little girl in Cantonese about not talking to strangers, then glared at Lily, Chase, and Olivia as they came through the bathroom door. As the mother pushed the stroller into the bathroom, Olivia heard her complaining about Americans using restrooms for their deviant sexual practices within the vicinity of decent people. Then a string of colorful and creative phrases followed as she realized that her stroller had rolled through Chase's vomit.

Olivia's anxiety wound tighter. She didn't want any innocent people hurt. Worse, she had no idea how they were going to get out of this, let alone how they would get out of Macau. Never mind what Starling planned for her that required using that sociopath, Lily.

Olivia took Chase's hand. She didn't know what was going to happen to them now.

The last became clear soon enough. They'd entered the gallery with the display of ceramics that Lily had quizzed the four-year-old about.

Liú Xiù, who'd been studying a blue-and-white porcelain vase, turned an inscrutable gaze on them. Olivia sensed more than saw the SSSB agents who blocked the exits but didn't enter the gallery with them.

The three of them halted in front of glass-enclosed shelves displaying numerous vases like the one with which Liú Xiù appeared engrossed.

Each fragile piece had the same large figure painted on the front. Inside what looked like a rayed sun were the letters I, H, and S. A cross, some actually a crucifix, stood on the crossbar of the H. The sign next to the display said that these formed the monogram of the Society of Jesus, the Jesuits, and the ceramics came from around the world.

"An interesting choice for meeting," said the Blue Widow, glancing at Olivia.

"It's public yet quiet," said Olivia.

Lily was smart enough to understand what had just happened. The power dynamics had just shifted out of her favor.

It was the most dangerous moment of the entire pear-shaped mission.

Lily laughed, sending a spike of pain through Olivia's left eye. She tensed, expecting violence and blood to erupt.

Instead, Lily said, "How appropriate! Uncle's little pet really is a Chinese minion! Those photos I took of you meeting with this cool Chinese bitch captured the real deal. You're a traitorous whore."

Ignoring Lily, Liú Xiù smiled at Olivia and Chase. "I thought that Mr. Graham was in charge. I see that I underestimated you, Ms. Markham."

Olivia dipped her chin and waited.

"Please." The Blue Widow gestured with an open palm for them to continue their tour. As they walked, she said, "Tell me, Ms. Markham, how did you know that I would find you and Ms. Crane here?"

Olivia shrugged. "I didn't. But since I knew that you were watching her as well as us, I figured there was a good chance that you would show up when we were both together."

Lily stopped, forcing Chase to halt. "This little *tête-à-tête* is all well and good, but you're talking to the wrong woman," she said to Liú Xiù. "You should be talking to the woman with the gun." She brandished the weapon, a terrible smile splitting her long face.

The Blue Widow struck like a cobra, if a cobra performed ballet.

She grabbed the gun's muzzle, leaning out of the trajectory of the bullet that Lily reflexively shot. At the same time Liú Xiù's other hand came up behind the gun, pulling it down and around towards Lily, who screamed as her trigger finger snapped audibly and her knees buckled. An instant later, Liú Xiù took possession of the 9mm, tapped its clip with the palm of her hand, and racked a bullet into the chamber. She aimed it with two unwavering hands at Lily's head.

The whole sequence took about two seconds. The stray bullet had gone into the ceiling, and Lily had been effectively taken out of commission. All with barely a ripple in the air around them.

The name *Liú Xiù* meant 'elegant kill.' It was apt.

At a slight dip of the Blue Widow's delicate chin, two SSSB agents descended upon Lily. While she spluttered and struggled, they dragged her from the gallery.

The enigmatic Chinese operative lowered the weapon as soon as Lily had been removed from her presence. She never spared a glance for the injured American CIA officer or Chase. Instead, she handed the weapon to one of the other SSSB agents and began gliding through the gallery again. Olivia had no choice but to follow at her side.

Another SSSB agent held up a hand in silent warning to Chase, who would have joined Olivia and Liú Xiù. Olivia shook her head when she caught his gaze.

Liú Xiù stopped in front of a case displaying the 1662 manuscript of the Commitment of the Holy House of Mercy, the original purpose of the historic building.

"You know Ms. Crane." It wasn't a question. "Yet you did not expect to see her when I showed you her photo."

Olivia held her breath and said nothing, simply nodded.

"She is not your equal. Whoever sent her fears you greatly or would not have chosen such a blunt instrument or chosen failure for such an important mission."

Olivia felt like she walked on an impossibly high tightrope over a deep chasm. Something told her that a lie here would be fatal. "It appears that he would prefer to burn me than keep me in play against the terrorists who buy Abadi's surface-to-air missiles."

Liú Xiù smiled again and continued. "We detained Mr. Abadi after you left the MGM. He did not have the jewelry." She watched Olivia from the side of her eye as she delivered this news.

Olivia's heart jumped when she heard it. "I don't know what you're talking about," she said carefully.

It wasn't a lie. She didn't know where the jewelry was if Abadi didn't have it.

"Perhaps Ms. Crane's handler thought to burn you in more than one way," said the Blue Widow. "After all, Mr. Graham opened accounts for a particular charity, did he not? A charity that would be most unhappy to have its 'charitable donation' routed elsewhere."

It rang true.

Olivia suddenly understood how Starling would spin a romantic tale of Bonnie and Clyde, international spy version, for Langley. There was plenty of photographic evidence of her and Graham together that could be misinterpreted to suit his story.

And plenty that supported it, no spin necessary. Sam, the discredited handler, had chosen poorly. His young recruit and her traitorous boyfriend had betrayed Hamas *and* the United States.

No wonder she'd sold out to Chinese intelligence. She couldn't go home or anywhere that Hamas could reach. Starling had tied everything up neatly.

Then Olivia fully comprehended what the Blue Widow had told her.

"Lily has the jewelry," she said slowly, realizing it was true as she said it.

Liú Xiù, who'd been watching her closely, smiled. "I see that you took off the jewelry that Mr. Graham bought you in the hotel gift shop," she said in apparent non sequitur. "That small medal suits you much better."

Olivia touched the St. Michael medal, having forgotten that she again wore it. It warmed in response.

Liú Xiù went on. "We have a mutual friend. It is because of him that I also wear a medal like yours." She touched her finger to her chest but didn't reveal the small disc beneath her blouse.

"I suggest that you do not dawdle in leaving Macau, Ms. Markham. The MGM holds your belongings, which you left behind in your haste to shop at the Venetian. You will also find that your helicopter flight at two p.m. will not wait for you."

Olivia heard the threads of submerged meaning in the Blue Widow's words, but she had no way to decode them. Something told her that she must just trust that the Chinese operative intended to let her and Chase leave the island.

She pressed her hands together and bowed at the waist, a deep show of respect and gratitude. "Thank you," she said in Mandarin.

Liú Xiù reciprocated. As Olivia turned to go, she said, "And Ms. Markham?"

Olivia paused and looked back, a question on her face. "You *do* have time for a stop between the Venetian and the Outer Harbor Ferry terminal, should you find a need for it."

Olivia bowed again, uncertain what largesse the Chinese operative had just bequeathed to her, but certain that it would prove useful if she could discover what clue Liú Xiù had left for her.

Gratitude for the unexpected aid filled her. She had no idea why the other woman had saved her life, but she had.

Olivia and Chase rode in silence in a taxi that one of the SSSB agents hailed for them across from Senado Square. The driver had clearly been instructed where to go and been paid in advance. He didn't speak to or look at them. They'd barely exited the backseat before he drove away.

Olivia didn't spare a thought for Lily. Whatever happened to the ambitious and unscrupulous field officer, she more than merited. And it was no worse than what Olivia would have done to her if given the chance.

Inside the Venetian, the concierge met Olivia and Chase with a ticket for their bags, which waited inside a locked room. After Olivia gave the ticket to the attendant, he left them alone.

Olivia went to her suitcase and toppled it on its side. As she unzipped it, Chase spoke at last.

"What are you doing? Shouldn't we get out of here as fast as we can?"

"I'm looking for whatever it is that Liú Xiù put in our luggage." Olivia continued searching through the dresses that Mousa had made Chase pack for her.

"She put something in our luggage?" asked Chase in alarm.

Olivia said nothing while she continued to search methodically through all of the clothes and shoes and even the cosmetic bag.

She'd nearly given up and turned to Chase's suitcase when something made her stop and return to the cosmetic bag, a rather ostentatious affair that she would never have carried as a private citizen but that the vain girlfriend of a wealthy investment manager would. There were some extra bottles of shampoo and conditioner from the hotel sundries shop that she hadn't purchased.

Slipping one free, she unscrewed the cap and sniffed.

Hm. Lavender and vanilla. Not her scent at all. She suspected that Liú Xiù somehow knew that.

Frowning, she squeezed the bottle, which seemed a little heavier than it should. Shampoo squirted everywhere.

But in squeezing the bottle, Olivia had gotten her answer. Sitting back on her heels, she dug into her go bag, into the secret compartment in the bottom where she'd packed a set of lockpicking tools. Removing a long thin tool, she dipped it into the shampoo bottle and fished out a milky tendril that ended in a heavy white glob, which she wiped on her pants.

Then she held up the ridiculous diamond that she'd been forced to wear last night to the poker table when meeting Abadi.

She looked up to Chase's stunned face. "Yes, I'd say she left us our way back home."

ELEVEN

Olivia and Chase arrived back in the United States via Seattle using the false passports they procured in Hong Kong. Tess had proven a useful double agent, having satisfied Langley's questions about Sam and, as it turned out, Olivia. She was the one who'd alerted Fiona that Olivia had made it onto an internal CIA watchlist, which meant that her passport—and likely Chase's—had been flagged within the domestic air-travel system. Then Tess sent crucial information gleaned from CIA resources about Hong Kong document packagers to Fiona, who'd passed it to Olivia.

Sam was still in the wind, and Tara, though she'd been the one to pass along the information about Hong Kong resources to Tess, had apparently cut ties with her former teammates. Since her father, uncle, brothers, and several cousins all still served active duty in various branches of the military, it made sense. She wasn't going to let a charge of treason sully her unblemished service record.

Julia and Monica, unaware of the crisis when they arrived in Hong Kong, had boarded a flight to the U.S. whose final leg took them to

D.C. where someone from the CIA met them at the gate. They were still being debriefed at Langley when Olivia and Chase touched down on American soil on the opposite coast.

In Hong Kong, Olivia and Chase had changed their appearance at the packager's site, above a noodle shop far from the tourist areas. Both darkened their hair, though Olivia, recalling the nondescript "German" traveler from her flight home in June, had only sought a less bright blond color. When they arrived on U.S. soil, they had become French-Canadian citizens from Quebec named Luc and Danielle Martin, who were laying over on a flight to Quebec, where they changed their appearance yet again and drove across the Canadian border as Mark and Ava Gardiner to the suburbs of Boston.

Olivia, who'd never spent much time away from home before, needed to check in with her family, even if it meant sneaking in while they were gone. She longed to stroke Oliver's velvety ears and hold a loudly purring Alfred in her arms. She'd inhale her mother's perfume, embedded in her pillow, and bury her face in her father's favorite Notre Dame sweatshirt, the one with fraying cuffs. She even planned to wander through Michael and Dianne's rooms.

What she got instead was a cold dose of reality.

Several black Escalades blocked the driveway with two more parked on the street. The front door had been left open, and several dark-suited men carried items from the house. Two men stood outside with their hands crossed, one on the sidewalk and one in the street. Oliver, half deaf and stiff with arthritis, broke free of the man holding his leash. He snarled and barked at the intruders, going so far as to nip at one's heels.

Olivia and Chase, who'd parked on a side street and watched from the back of the Paulsens' house, saw the man kick Oliver. Hard.

Olivia heard the *thud* of his shod foot against Oliver's side, heard the sharp *yelp*. Saw her beloved golden retriever fly a few feet to land on his side. Saw him struggle to rise and then collapse again.

Hot tears sheeted her face.

But she pulled her burner phone out and called 911, praying that whoever came would take Oliver to the vet. That the loyal companion of her childhood wouldn't be irredeemably injured.

That her family wouldn't be put through any more, not now. Not after Emily and Ibiza.

Mrs. Paulsen had grimmer news when Olivia rang her doorbell as the sound of sirens shrilled through the quiet October afternoon.

"Olivia?" she asked, blinking in confusion. "I thought you were in Maryland. What did you do to your lovely hair?"

Then the older woman looked across at Olivia's house as two police cars pulled in behind the Escalades. "Come inside, dear. No need for you to get pulled into whatever is happening there."

Mrs. Paulsen insisted on feeding them lunch while she told them it was her fault that Olivia's parents were being investigated. She didn't understand it, but it had something to do with her son-in-law and his work at the FBI. She was sure the reason her grandchildren's father had been whisked away was because she'd asked him to waste FBI resources earlier in the summer.

Guilt-ridden, Olivia put her hand on the older woman's and assured her that it couldn't be so simple. Then she asked Mrs. Paulsen to keep her visit a secret. She'd only come home to pick something up and didn't want to worry her parents.

Mrs. Paulsen, who'd looked fretful, turned a suddenly firm gaze on Olivia. "Of course! There's no reason for those assholes"—she lifted her chin in the direction of the dark-suited men—"to learn you were here."

Olivia, clasping her medal and wishing *Sensei* Mark was there with her, waited long enough to see Oliver being carried by a patrolman to his car. Something caused the dog to look toward the Paulsens' and wag his tail.

Olivia and Chase left before the Escalades and their terrible crew, the local police having been dismissed almost as soon as they arrived. Then, after another stop, they flew from Logan to D.C.

Three days after learning that Starling had set them up, Olivia and Chase ended their journey.

Fiona picked them up at Dulles late that night and drove them to the bedroom community of Leesburg, northwest of the airport and capital. There she'd rented a basement studio apartment in a family home that had its own entrance in back through a sunroom, making it easy for them to come and go without much notice.

Fiona turned on the lights in the tiny kitchen while Chase and Olivia waited in the darkened living room. As she dropped her back-pack on the banquette table in the corner, she said, "The hair color is all wrong, Liv. You look too much like me."

"Duly noted," said Olivia, exhausted and defeated.

She sat on the padded bench against the wall under the table. They'd hardly had any sleep in the past 96 hours, and it was finally taking a toll on her. She felt dull and heavy, like an old wet dishrag.

Chase also sat down on the other end of the bench and propped his head in his hands, which he scrubbed over his face. He'd barely said anything since Macau, but he'd played his part when necessary.

Fiona filled a teakettle and set it on the stove. When Olivia started to protest, she said in her no-nonsense way, "We still have to go over some basics before you two can crash. And tea will actually help ease you to sleep."

Olivia, the older sister herself, yawned against the back of her hand. "Yes, Mom."

As Fiona set mugs on the table, the door to the porch opened, and Tess came in.

"Hey, Liv, you look like shit," she said, rough affection in her voice as she bent over to hug Olivia.

"That's okay," said Olivia. "I feel like it, too."

Tess lifted her chin with a "hey" for Chase before she leaned against the sideboard. Now the tiny kitchen seemed crowded. Aware of the family living in the main house, everyone moved and spoke quietly.

Tess went on. "Fiona told me about your visit home. I can't believe those assholes at Langley packing up your stuffed animals and ribbons."

Chase, who'd been toying with the handle of his mug, said, "Don't forget kicking her dog and terrorizing her family."

Olivia felt a rush of gratitude for Chase. She had no idea what was going to happen between them, but his brief acknowledgement of her pain helped ease the tightness between her shoulders.

Still, she shrugged and sipped her tea. "They're just doing their jobs. Starling's done a good job of making me look like a traitor, which is one small step below terrorist."

Car doors sounded outside, and they stilled. Fifteen seconds later, Julia and Monica walked in. The shadows and puffiness on their faces attested to the grueling interviews they'd endured during their recent debriefing.

Swallowing an exclamation, Olivia got up and hugged both women.

After everyone had settled into a seat or corner of the living room, all gazes turned to Olivia.

Right. She'd been the lead on this mission, and her actions with Chase in Macau had come under suspicion because of Starling.

Inhaling, she closed her eyes and then looked around at all of her teammates. "First, I want to thank you all for being here. I wasn't sure what I would come back to."

No one said anything, just waited for her to continue.

"And I want to assure you that I'm not a traitor. I executed my mission with Chase faithfully."

Now Monica spoke for the rest of the team. She sat forward, her eyes narrowed and her gaze intent. "We know that, Olivia. We never doubted you for a second."

A lump rose in Olivia's throat so quickly that she had to swallow several times and blink the tears that came with it out of her eyes. She swiped them with her thumb before continuing.

"What you don't know is that I knew that Starling is dirty from the outset. He's running ghost assets and pocketing the money that the CIA pays for them." She paused as the others took in that news. "He also sent Lily to Macau to steal the jewelry from Abadi and frame us."

The other women nodded. They'd gotten the manipulated details from their CIA interviews.

"What about Uncle?" asked Julia. "How does he factor into all of this? Why burn him? I thought he and Starling were tight."

Olivia started to shrug when Fiona said, "I think we can let Uncle answer that for himself."

An almost visible thrum ran through the living room as everyone sat up a little, opening their eyes wide.

Fiona went to the slider to the sunroom, opened it, and said, "Ok, you can come in, Uncle. The team's assembled and waiting for you."

A shiver raced down Olivia's spine. She'd heard nothing, not even the outside door to the porch, to alert her to his presence. Given everyone else's expressions, neither had they.

A moment later Sam appeared in the room. His unshaven face would have looked haggard except for the burning, hard gaze that looked at each one of them. He arrived at Olivia last.

"You got out of Macau quickly. Good work, Markham," he said.

"Thanks. It wasn't easy. Lily Crane planned to make our stay permanent." Olivia didn't have to say that Lily had tried to kill them.

Sam's gaze blazed at her announcement. Monica and Fiona muttered, but Tess just crossed her arms while Julia narrowed her eyes. She in particular had never liked Lily, who'd aimed at her as chief rival until Olivia showed up at Eagle's Nest.

"What are we going to do about this, Uncle?" asked Monica. "That prick Starling practically named all of us as co-conspirators unless we turned on Olivia. Is that why he burned you, to keep you from fighting this?"

Sam, his lips compressed, nodded. "He knew his shitty little tale would never fly with me. I've never had a defective pick before, unlike him with Crane. He also knew that I was starting to get suspicious about some of his activities. What better way to kill two birds with one stone than by hanging his crimes on me?"

Sam sounded bitter. Olivia wondered if it was more than being falsely accused. She'd never trusted Starling, but it had seemed as if he and Sam had a longstanding relationship.

Sam went on. "I can take care of myself. But I'll never forgive that bastard for what he's done to my team. What he's done to Olivia." He turned to her. "I'll make sure you have a complete, impeccable identity package. You can stay safely in the U.S. while I work some connections on your behalf. But you're done at the Company as long as Starling's version of the truth stands."

Sam looked at the others. "As for the rest of you, stick to your guns. You don't need to fall in line with Starling's claims. It might take a while, but I know you'll be cleared to work again. Just not together."

A heavy silence descended.

Until Olivia broke it. "No. That's not good enough."

Everyone's gazes swiveled to her, stunned.

Olivia played with the St. Michael medal. It warmed against her fingertips.

"Starling doesn't get to win. That makes him as bad as the terrorists. Worse. He's flying a false flag as an intelligence officer of the United States. I refuse to go down without a fight."

For a long moment, an inscrutable expression dominated Sam's face, and his eyes glittered. Then he smiled and leaned back, crossing his arms.

"That's my girl," he said, respect tempering the affection in his voice. "That's the warrior princess I saw on the beach at Ibiza that day. The one who said she was going to make the terrorists hurt before she went down."

Sam understood her then. "Exactly."

He nodded. "I'm in. But the rest of you"—he lifted his chin at everyone else sitting quietly around the living room—"you should scat. You don't want to be anywhere near Olivia and me now."

Monica, who stared at her nails as she spoke, said, "I disagree." Then she looked up and held Sam's gaze. "I've no intention of going anywhere. And I don't think anyone else does either."

"I'm staying here," said Julia as Fiona and Tess chimed in with "I'm not leaving" and "no way in hell does the princess get to have all the fun."

Sam's grin erased the fatigue on his handsome face. "That's the badass team I assembled at Eagle's Nest." Then the grin evaporated. "But there's little we can do. Starling holds most of the cards."

"*Mm*. Not the most important card," said Olivia, glancing at Chase, who'd sat up and listened to the shifting dynamics with submerged excitement.

There'd been no mention of his future.

Until now.

Sam had followed her glance. He sat forward, hands on his knees. "Go on, I'm listening."

"I have evidence of Starling's ghost assets. It's what I leveraged to get him to sponsor me at the Company," said Olivia, watching Sam's face.

Amazement lifted his eyes. "I've known for some time that he was padding his portfolio with false expenses, but I've had little success proving it."

That explained Sam's loyalty and apparent lack of judgment when it came to Starling.

"I won't ask how you, a civilian, came across this evidence," he said. "But that turns this from a bit of subversive retribution to a justified mission, albeit unsanctioned. I take it this evidence is something that Graham can help us with?"

Olivia nodded. "And Julia."

"That asshole doesn't know that Olivia and Chase made it back to the States," said Julia, chiming in. At her side, Monica made agreeing noises. "He asked all of us how fluent Olivia was in Mandarin, whether she had any connections in Macau, if we'd heard from her since she called the audible on the play."

"That answers at least one of my questions," said Olivia, sending a look of thanks at Julia and Monica. "And suggests that I scare the crap out of that bastard by showing up where he least expects me."

"I can lend a hand with that," said Fiona. "A little C-4 brings everyone to Jesus sooner or later. I prefer sooner."

Everyone except Chase grinned. Fiona was known for a fondness for explosions.

"Well, then, I think that it's time Uncle arranged a little cease-and-desist meeting with Starling," said Olivia, "the kind where he realizes that things might not be tied up as neatly as he thinks."

Sam, pressing his lips together, nodded. "I like what you're thinking. Rattle him a little. I bet you have ideas for what happens when he decides a show of force is necessary."

Olivia smiled. "A few." She glanced at Chase. "Time to send your tux to the dry cleaners, darling, and tell Mousa to bring his checkbook to the Strathmore community concert."

On Veteran's Day, the Strathmore Music Center hosted a special benefit concert for the Artist in Residence program that also included raising money for a scholarship for returning veterans who wanted to study music. The concert program, featuring AIR musicians, narrated a story from soaring cultural feeling for homeland to the personal and intimate love that led citizens to serve and the sacrifices that love required.

In the audience of nearly two thousand, Ghassan Mousa sat in a private balcony with a small group of donors from the local Muslim community, most of whom were being used as props to bolster Mousa's image of generous benefactor and steadfast American patriot.

On the main floor of the wood-paneled auditorium known for its pitch-perfect acoustics sat Larry Starling with Tara. Next to them, crisp in their beribboned dress uniforms, several Army soldiers clapped and whistled for every performance.

The concert opened with the classic hymn *America, the Beautiful* and the Irving Berlin standard *God Bless America* before moving to the recent country hit *God Bless the USA*. The jazzy *America* student chorus led into *America, My Country, 'Tis of Thee*, sung by special guests, the Army Field Band Soldiers Chorus. Then a student trio sang the World War Two-era popular song *This is My Country*. More songs followed, both earnestly serious and lighthearted.

After the rousing opening and spirited middle acts, a young baritone sang a somber country ballad, *Some Gave All*, that changed the tenor of the concert. After him, a bass performed Johnny Cash's spoken-word song, *Ragged Old Flag*. And just when the program had subdued the audience, a gospel choir sang René Marie's arrangement of *Lift Ev'ry Voice and Sing* set to *The Star-Spangled Banner*, releasing the solemn mood with an almost audible relief.

Charlotte Dunning came onto the stage. After the vigorous cheering subsided, she said, "We are so fortunate tonight to finish the concert with a special duet by one of the Institute's most devoted benefactors with one of Strathmore's most gifted new voices. Please welcome Mr. Chase Graham and Ms. Olivia Markham singing the

World War Two ballad *La Vie En Rose*. I can think of no sentiment more fitting to end our program in honor of our nation's veterans."

The audience quieted as Chase escorted Olivia, who wore the red gown that Mousa had sent for her to wear in Macau, onto the stage.

They sang the French lyrics to each other with heartfelt optimism, their mutual adoration clear in their every move and every measure of the song. But when they turned to the audience, their arms outstretched to embrace its members, they sang in English. They looked around, holding gazes with those in the nearest rows and smiling.

Olivia let her gaze trail indifferently over Mousa as if he didn't exist. Even so, she noted his scowl and repeated shifting in his seat.

When Starling came under her wandering survey, she stared at his impassive face, beaming at him with all the confidence that she didn't feel.

Fake it 'til you make it, Olivia.

After the song ended, a wistful, romantic mood hung over the hall like a promise. Then the audience erupted from their seats in delighted uproar, their enthusiastic approval deafening. Charlotte handed Olivia, who nodded graciously, a huge bouquet of long-stemmed roses.

She and Chase waved and left the stage, but the applause continued. They strode back, waving, and bowed again. Olivia threw kisses, seemingly to everyone, but her steady look returned to Starling, who still sat with Tara while those around him had risen to their feet.

This time, Olivia nodded, her smile gone and her eyes narrowed. *No kisses for you, you bastard.*

Starling dipped his chin, a hostile expression replacing the formerly unreadable one.

He'd gotten the message. She was here on a mission, and he was the target.

She and Chase turned and waved, strolling from the stage. The audience continued clapping.

But they didn't reappear, not even when all of the acts returned for one last round of applause.

TWELVE

That's because Tarek and Wael, the two members of the Black Hand, intercepted Olivia and Chase in the dark wings of the stage while the thunderous clapping and cheering covered their harsh commands and rough hands.

Olivia squelched the impulse to disarm Tarek, whose muzzle burrowed into the soft flesh of her lower back. She shot a look at Chase, who stumbled as Wael gripped his arm and jerked him toward the stairs to the exit door.

He shook his head at her mute question. He didn't need aid.

Tarek's hot breath assaulted the back of her neck as he leaned forward to speak into her ear. "Come, little songbird. Time for your swansong."

Then he jabbed the muzzle into her spine.

Olivia got the hint. She followed Chase and Wael out of the backstage area. In the brighter light of the hall, she realized that the two Hamas terrorists had dressed as concertgoers in suits, blending in with the handful of audience members leaving early before the crowd slowed their exit. Wael had moved alongside Chase as if they were old friends, his gun hidden for the moment, forcing Chase to move quickly before anyone recognized him and stopped them.

Olivia wasn't so lucky.

Tarek kept his hand on her lower back, his gun hand hidden under her large bouquet of long-stemmed roses, which he appeared to help her carry.

"Smile," he said to her. He continued in Palestinian Arabic. *Stupid whore, wearing that dress. You'll die in it.*

Olivia refrained from answering him, although anger surged, increasing her adrenaline. And clarified her thoughts into icy lucidity.

Outside the music center, the two Black Hand terrorists shoved Olivia and Chase into a waiting black Lincoln Navigator, forcing Olivia to drop her roses on the pavement.

They were clearly undaunted by possible detection. Then again, they'd grown bold after six unfettered weeks in D.C., the center of power for the primary global opponent of Islamic terrorism.

As Olivia ducked her head to get into the backseat with Tarek and Chase, she glimpsed Mousa outside the entrance. He appeared to be taking his leave of his guests, laughing and exchanging handshakes and kisses on both cheeks. But she knew that he would follow them. Mousa wouldn't want to miss his chance to express his disappointment in his "brother" Chase.

The Black Hand members hadn't bothered to jam black hoods over their heads. Wael took the Capital Beltway to 185 South. Olivia wasn't familiar with the route, but she knew that they'd headed into D.C. They got off at Connecticut Avenue. After a ten-minute drive, they pulled inside a black wrought-iron gate in front of a three-story limestone building with a red and dark-green flag hanging from a tall flagpole in front.

Obviously, an embassy. Not good. Embassies were sovereign land of the visiting nation.

Meaning U.S. laws—and U.S. authority—stopped at the edge of the property. Essentially making whomever it was that sheltered the Black Hand and Mousa untouchable.

Wael parked the SUV in front of the entrance. Tarek jumped out and came around to the other side, opening first Chase's door and then Olivia's. He gestured with his gun for them to get out. Once they had, Wael drove away.

Tarek hustled them toward the building where a short, dark-haired man in glasses and a suit waited inside the vestibule. The empty security desk attested to the conspiracy. Large serif letters spelled "Embassy of Bangladesh" over the glass-walled entrance.

Their guide led them down a long shallow staircase tiled in slate that opened up into a large gathering area. To the right, a door led into a conference room where the man left them. The air conditioning had been turned on high. Combined with her sleeveless gown, it raised gooseflesh on Olivia's exposed skin. She resisted rubbing her arms.

The embassy functionary nodded once at Tarek before leaving. The lock clicked.

"No plastic on the floor?" asked Olivia. Despite intending to convey humor, her question held an edge. The next few minutes were going to be some of the longest in her life. "Planning on killing us somewhere else then?"

Tarek ignored her.

She glanced at Chase, whose compressed lips and fine lines around his eyes told their own story. Then she assessed the room.

It was an interior room with no windows and a single access door.

Should she disarm Tarek and get out of here before anyone else arrived? They were like rats in a trap here. Her cold skin itched.

But she doubted she could overpower the terrorist, who watched her with a falcon's eyes. She'd need to wait for better odds.

After about ten minutes, the lock clicked again, and the door opened to reveal Wael and Mousa, who had removed his tie and unbuttoned his collar. Wael grinned, a gold dental overlay glinting in the fluorescent light. He looked like a denizen of Hell.

Mousa halted in front of them. He took off his jacket. Shaking his head, he handed it to Wael as he said, "Brother, I'm disappointed in you. Very disappointed."

Chase shifted next to Olivia. "Why are we here? I did everything you asked me to do." A defiant thread underscored his words.

Mousa unbuttoned his cuffs and began rolling his sleeves up. He was going to get his hands dirty then.

The Hamas front man paused. "Indeed? Our gift to the widows and orphans in Indonesia never got delivered. And our Egyptian friend never got payment for his goods. Our good Saudi friend never made it to Malaysia. In fact, he never left Macau. Yet your whore of a girlfriend wears my dress without its valuable gems. And you dare to invite me to hear you sing at that obscene paean to American hegemony."

Chase inhaled, his nostrils flaring. He straightened, anger in every line of his body. Olivia set her hand on his forearm.

"We gave Abadi the jewelry. Maybe he stole it from you," she said.

In response, Mousa struck her with an open palm.

Olivia's head snapped to the side. Jagged white light flashed through her vision, and her ears rang. She touched the tip of her tongue to the corner of her mouth. Blood.

Then she scowled. Of course, Mousa would go for what he believed was the most vulnerable of the pair.

She smiled at him. It didn't reach her eyes.

Mousa, who'd waited—presumably for her to waver or cry out—widened *his* eyes at her expression. Perhaps he wasn't as stupid as he seemed.

Time to let him know who really ran Chase.

"You must think yourself invulnerable inside the Bangladeshi embassy. Am I right?"

It was Tarek's turn to deliver a blow. He used the butt of his handgun on the back of her head. Olivia crumpled to her knees, her head dipping. Pain made tears spring from her eyes. Inhaling sharply, she squeezed them. Then she pushed herself to a squat before rising to her feet.

She ignored Mousa to look at Tarek. "And you think you can come to the U.S. capital and act with impunity." She let a slight dismissive sneer curl the corner of her mouth.

When Tarek would have struck her again, Mousa held out a hand.

"Who are you?" he asked. All three terrorists focused on her.

"Someone who knows it isn't wise to trust in friends whose country fears the U.S. Did you really believe that you had safe harbor here? That the Bangladeshis would tolerate you killing U.S. citizens?" Olivia paused to let her words sink in. As Mousa and the Black Hand terrorists shifted, looking at one another, she said, "Go!"

Several things happened at once.

Chase dropped to the floor.

Olivia stepped inside Tarek's reach, slamming the heel of her hand upward into his jaw. She followed it with a knee to his groin. As he doubled, she rammed her elbow into his temple before disarming him. By the time he recovered, she held his own weapon in unwavering aim at his head.

The door burst open. Fiona ran in, squeezing off a shot at Wael, who'd spun to face the door and raised his weapon too late. Monica came in after and sighted on Mousa, who bent to yank Chase to his feet.

Before he could use Chase as a shield, Monica said, "Uh-uh-uh. We don't want to leave our Bangladeshi friends a mess to clean up."

Sam followed behind his team. He was unarmed and strolled toward Mousa. As he pulled out zip cuffs and jerked the terrorist's arms behind his back, he said, "Take it from me, 'brother,' it's not wise to pigeonhole women, especially one who's already survived an attack by killing terrorists with their own weapons."

A few days later, Olivia returned to the Bethesda apartment that she, Monica, and Julia had shared for a few brief weeks. Not much of her belongings remained after Langley's investigators had gotten through with them. She'd left most of what she cared about at home, but she suspected that even that had been taken. She looked around the bedroom that she'd spent so little time in, an ache in her heart and a lump in her throat at the callous disarray. Clothes had been dumped from drawers and hangers, shoes toppled in odd places, the bedding stripped, and cherished mementos scattered, broken, or lost.

She felt like something had been stolen from her, something that she'd never get back.

Olivia knelt to pick up the ripped bear wearing a doctor's outfit that her cousin Emily had made for her sixteenth birthday at that popular place in the mall. She'd turned 21 two days ago, but it had barely registered. She felt much older already.

"Time to leave your childhood behind," said Starling from the doorway.

Fury combusted inside her chest, but Olivia only squeezed the bear. The faint scent of Emily's perfume wafted to her. Her St. Michael medal radiated against her skin, pressed there by the stuffed animal. She set the bear gently on the bed and stood, turning to face the opponent she always knew she'd have to face if she wanted to succeed as an intelligence officer.

She'd just thought it would take a lot longer.

She folded her arms across her chest and studied the man who'd recruited her but said nothing to his petty taunt. Emily's memory deserved better.

Starling looked much the same as he had at their last team meeting: tall, lean, with iron-gray hair, eerie light eyes, and deep brackets around his pressed lips. He didn't blink but held her gaze for some time. He had her trapped. He thought she'd yield under his stare.

When it became clear that his hostile gaze failed to penetrate her defenses, Starling at last said, "Nice play with Mousa and his two goons. The Company suddenly finds it difficult to believe that you sold the U.S. out in Macau and ran away with your wealthy lover after you show up in D.C. and gift wrap terrorists for them. In fact, there're rumors that upper-level management has plans for you."

Olivia tipped her chin acknowledging Starling's words.

Starling shifted and reached into his pocket to pull out a 9mm and the distinctive bore of a silencer, which he screwed onto the muzzle as he asked, "What happened to Crane? She never reported back from Macau."

Olivia did her best to ignore the Sig Sauer. She shrugged. "The SSSB picked her up." She tilted her head and pursed her lips. "You should be grateful. She had no intention of sharing the two million dollars with you."

Starling sighed dramatically, but his aim never wavered. "That's always the risk you run when you trust ambitious underlings. I guess I have you to thank for taking care of that little problem?"

He laughed. It sent chills down Olivia's spine.

"Not really," she said. "Like you, Crane was overconfident and didn't recognize her vulnerabilities."

That caught Starling's attention. Narrowing his eyes, he stood upright. Cheeks flushed, he asked, "Still trying to play the game, Markham? You may have outmaneuvered me at The Company, but you're out of moves. It ends here."

He raised the Sig Sauer.

"Indeed, it does," said Sam behind him, his own weapon aimed in a two-handed grip at the back of Starling's head. "Hello, Yesterday. Looks like you got caught up in the past."

Starling lowered his own weapon and shifted to look over his shoulder at his former team commander.

"Ahren," he said with a brusque nod. "I wondered when you'd show up. Your fingerprints were all over the op at the Bangladesh Embassy. Nice work redeeming your team."

"Actually, that was Olivia's idea," said Sam, gesturing for Starling to hand him his weapon, "Funny thing, the CIA got some new information about that Bahamas bank account that put my ownership in doubt."

Starling flashed a sharp grin at Olivia as he handed the Sig Sauer to Sam. "I always wondered if you really had the goods on me or just a rumor from an ex-Spec-Ops friend."

"That's the thing, Starling," said Sam accepting the 9mm. "You never know who has what against you when you're out for yourself. Seems you made a few enemies along the way."

He offered Starling's gun to Olivia, who took it, checked the clip, and then aimed it at the glowering CIA officer while Sam handcuffed him.

"In fact," said Olivia, lifting her chin at Sam to signal that they were good to move out, "we have some friends who're very interested in your extracurriculars."

Starling shrugged, unimpressed. He walked into the living room of the apartment, Olivia following. "I've got quite a few friends myself."

"Hope you don't mean me," said Tara, entering from the kitchen. She grinned at Starling's shocked face. "Sorry to disappoint you, but I'm not here as your backup. When I said I had your six, I had my fingers crossed behind my back. I was really making sure you made it to the meeting without any other support."

She was dressed in black tactical clothing and wore an earpiece. She looked at Sam. "Our guests are here, sir."

"Right on time," said Sam, directing Starling to the small breakfast table where Olivia, Monica, Julia, and he had planned mission tactics. "Have a seat. I'd offer you a drink, but it's not that kind of meeting."

When Starling halted several feet away and refused to sit, Tara stepped forward and kicked the back of his knee. He lurched. She shoved him into a seat on the couch. Starling glared at her.

Then he fixed a hard stare on Sam. "Whatever you've got planned, it won't work," he said. "Barnes here isn't my only friend. And it'll take more than questionable bank-account ownership to resolve the ghost assets for the Company. Someone has to pay. At best you've only delayed the inevitable, Ahren."

Now Sam grinned, his teeth bright in his tanned face. "Really? Wow. How much was it again that I stole from the U.S. taxpayers? Five million dollars? Sounds like a tidy little nest egg, even without the two million in jewelry your protégé Crane planned to steal from you. But what are *you* going to retire on? I'm pretty sure you won't be able to run the same con again. Oh, I know. Maybe this time the Quds Force can pay you two million dollars to negotiate a deal for SAMs to target Israel."

Before Starling could respond, a knock came at the door. Tara answered it. A hard-looking couple entered, a tall, thin female and a shorter, muscular male. Their olive skin and brown hair gave them a Mediterranean cast. When they stopped just inside the apartment door, the male's jacket moved to reveal a holstered weapon.

Starling narrowed his eyes, scooting forward on the couch and straightening as best he could with hands bound behind his back.

"Who're they?" he demanded.

Everyone else ignored him.

The female addressed Sam. "Your tip checks out, Ahren. We'll take him now." She nodded at her partner, who strode to Starling and jerked him to his feet.

Starling struggled against his escort's grip until the male's gaze sparked. Before he could pull his weapon, however, Sam held a palm up.

"Wait. I'm sure Yesterday will go with you once he understands his situation."

The female looked at him a moment before nodding at her partner.

Sam looked at Olivia. "Would you do the honors, Markham? You're the one who alerted us to Yesterday's asset's activity in Macau."

Olivia, who'd watched the scene play out with growing satisfaction, smiled when Starling's gaze whipped to hers. She saw when he started to put all of the pieces together.

"Of course, Uncle," she said, never looking away from Starling. "As close allies with Israel, we've given Mossad access to the private investment account that Yesterday's asset opened at Citibank Macau."

Yesterday's eyes bulged. He spluttered, but the male hit him once, hard.

Olivia continued. "They've already confirmed its links with the fake Indonesian charity set up to pay Kader as well as identified the jewelry left in a safe deposit box there as the pieces Mousa supplied."

Time for the *coup d'grâce*.

"In exchange for taking you off the Company's payroll"—Olivia grinned at her euphemism—"Mossad will share what it has on the *hawaladar* network in Southeast Asia. A win-win, don't you think?"

The following May Olivia traveled home after finishing a semester fulltime at the National Intelligence Defense College. Though she still had three semesters to go before earning a college degree, she'd already been cleared for additional specialized training in languages at the Farm as well as training with Special Operations Forces outside of the CIA. She'd spend another year fulltime at NIDC, then finish up whatever remaining courses she needed over the summers so that she could start official CIA 101.

One of the benefits of Olivia's unorthodox entry into Clandestine Services was that the Assistant Director intended to use her on a long-term internal investigation into the Special Activities Division, which had been a key component in Starling's ability to run ghost assets. He'd worked with Spec-Ops recruits to create a blizzard of fake paperwork and byzantine verification trails until it would take the most dedicated and gifted bureaucrat to ferret out the falsehoods.

Sam and the rest of the two teams, Alpha and Bravo, continued on missions that benefited from their unique makeup, which largely meant Western European assignments. Although Olivia officially dropped out of Strathmore, she stayed on as Monica and Julia's roommate. Though she was never read in on their missions, Olivia nevertheless shared in the general buzz of excitement whenever they prepped for action and celebrated when they came home. She hoped that someday she too would travel to Europe for fieldwork.

She hadn't seen Chase again except as she passed him in the hallway after his debriefing at Langley. He avoided looking at her. Even though Olivia knew he was grateful that she'd managed to disentangle him from Mousa, turning him into a former CIA asset instead of a candidate for treason, it stung a little.

Later, after her CIA record had been cleared and before she plunged into her studies at NIDC, Olivia had called Chase. The phone rang several times, and she was just about to hang up when Chase answered.

"You didn't need to call," he said without preamble. "We both know that our relationship was like a hothouse rose. It was never going to survive your mission."

"That's not fair. You make it sound like I used you," said Olivia, reeling a little.

Chase's audible sigh belied his next words.

"Didn't you?" he asked, although gently. "And you'd do it again if the CIA needed it. While I, on the other hand, welcomed the distraction from the mess I'd gotten myself in. Neither is a recipe for success. Let's just agree that our futures diverge—you to become a badass spy and me to learn to live without always looking over my shoulder."

And Olivia was forced to accept that their romance, such as it was, was indeed done.

This Memorial Day, she'd joined her family at their favorite Cape Cod cottage, the one her parents had rented for years. Dianne, who'd just finished her freshman year at UMass-Amherst, had invited several of her college friends, including her current boyfriend, to camp out in the tiny backyard. Michael, still in high school, couldn't believe he'd been forced to spend the whole weekend with his family. Neither sibling really paid attention to Olivia.

Her parents knew that she'd enrolled at NIDC, but she'd told them only that she intended to work in some capacity for the CIA. They didn't ask any probing questions, and she didn't volunteer any specifics. After what had happened last fall, they'd understood that Olivia wasn't free to say more.

It left a wistful distance between her and her parents.

Olivia strolled down to the beach, letting the sound of the surf and the smell of the ocean take her back, briefly, to her childhood. She and Emily, the same age, had escaped the younger cousins every chance they got.

After this weekend, Olivia didn't know when—or if—she'd ever be back.

"Emily," she said, tears misting her vision and thickening her voice, "I miss you."

She fell silent, at a loss for words.

A shadow fell on the sand as someone blocked the setting sun behind her.

Sensei Mark came to stand at Olivia's side.

"It's beautiful," he said, folding his arms across his chest.

Olivia, who'd arranged to see her mentor during this visit home, felt better as soon as he joined her. It was as if he'd taken some of her pain and shared its burden. She sighed and wished Emily's soul peace.

"Thank you for all your help," she said, not looking at her mentor until she continued, "I couldn't have done it without you."

Sensei Mark bowed his head. After a moment, he said, "You're still wearing the pendant I gave you."

Olivia looked down. Laughing, she lifted the pendant from her chest. "You know, it's funny. It comforts me on dangerous missions. It reminds me of you. All the sudden, I'll think about it. And then I don't lose focus."

He looked at her then, twisting a little to face her. He reached for the pendant. Holding it between thumb and forefinger, he said, "You can have it blessed by a priest, if you want."

Olivia shook her head. "I'm not really a believer, *Sensei*. You can bless it. That would mean more to me anyway."

"As you wish," he said. Then bowing his head again, he murmured a few words too low for Olivia to make out even though her exceptional hearing had blown away the CIA doctor.

Then *Sensei* Mark did something unexpected. Holding her face, he kissed Olivia on the forehead. It tingled, as if something more than lips had pressed against her skin.

He drew back, and his brilliant blue gaze captured hers.

"I'm proud of you, Olivia. Never forget who you are or what your true mission is. When in doubt, listen to your conscience and think of me."

Mutely, Olivia nodded, bowing when her karate teacher bowed. She watched as he walked away down the beach, the vast restless ocean on one side and the shadowy grass-covered dunes on the other.

Even though she had no idea if she'd ever see her mentor again, she'd somehow been left with a deep sense of peace and an unshakeable purpose.

ABOUT THE AUTHOR

Liane Zane is the cover identity of a novelist who is an expert at hiding in plain sight. She has spent time interrogating a former Army intelligence officer and engaging in Open Source Intelligence (OSINT) activities related to Italian slang words for naughty body parts and the proclivities of Eastern European criminals. She spends her days drinking New England chocolate-raspberry coffee and gazing at the magical brook in her back yard as she plots her romantic thrillers or walking her monstrous dog along mountain trails near her estate-like home.

THE COVERT GUARDIAN (Book One) is the first book in Liane's new series, THE UNSANCTIONED GUARDIANS, which narrates the genesis of the Wild *Elioud* (Olivia, Beta, and Stasia) from THE ELIOUD LEGACY into a disciplined team of covert advocates for innocent victims, especially of sex trafficking and assault. THE ELIOUD LEGACY comprises THE HARLEQUIN & THE DRANGÙE (Olivia & Mihàil's story), THE FLOWER & THE BLACKBIRD (Stasia & Miró's story), and THE DRAKA & THE

GIANT (Beta and András's story). All three books tell the complex legacy of the *Elioud* descendants of the Fallen Watcher Angels and are therefore best read in order.

Visit www.lianezane.com for updates and to buy merchandise related to the series.

ALSO BY

The Elioud Legacy

The Harlequin & The Drangùe

The Flower & The Blackbird

The Draka & The Giant

The Unsanctioned Guardians (prequel to The *Elioud* Legacy)
The Covert Guardian
The Harlequin Protocol (forthcoming)

Available in paperback, ebook, and audiobook online at all major retailers or through your local library by request. Check the copyright page for the ISBN numbers to expedite ordering.